Editors' Notes to Accompany

FOURTH EDITION

SIGNS OF LIFE
IN THE USA

Readings on Popular Culture for Writers

Sonia Maasik   Jack Solomon

Copyright © 2003 by Bedford/St. Martin's

All rights reserved.
Manufactured in the United States of America.

7 6 5 4 3 2
f e d c b a

For information, write: Bedford/St. Martin's, 75 Arlington Street, Boston, MA 02116 (617-399-4000)

ISBN: 0-312-39786-0

Instructors who have adopted *Signs of Life in the U.S.A.,* Fourth Edition, as a textbook for a course are authorized to duplicate portions of this manual for their students.

PREFACE

We realize that few instructors sit down and read an entire text cover-to-cover before designing their syllabi. You simply don't have the time, and doing so would likely interfere with your ability to adjust your course to your students' interests and needs. And we also realize that most instructors roam around in the texts they use, jumping from chapter to chapter and selecting some readings while skipping others. Accordingly, we've designed this instructor's manual to make it easier for you to plan your course. We suggest possible ways to combine chapters to form a coherent unit and ways to abbreviate chapters should you not have time to cover all the readings in each. We suggest thematic links that run throughout *Signs of Life*, links that may not always be apparent in the selections' titles. And we suggest ways to sequence your discussion of the readings so your students can build on their experience addressing other topics.

But the manual doesn't just organize the material in the text; we've also designed it to suggest how you can use *Signs of Life* in the classroom. Perhaps most important, we explain why we've chosen to make a theoretical approach explicit in a reader for composition students and why we've adopted semiotics as that approach. We also anticipate students' responses to the issues raised in *Signs of Life*. This text is based on widespread classroom experience, as we've received ample feedback from instructors across the nation who've used the previous three editions of *Signs of Life*. In addition, we've assigned many of the readings ourselves, and we've both adopted a semiotic approach in teaching students at different levels. Thus, by identifying which essays are likely to anger or excite students, which selections are relatively difficult or easy to read, which topics are perfect for personal reflection, and so forth, we can help you to devise a class plan that will work for *your* students.

In addition, we suggest activities beyond essay writing that will enhance students' understanding of the issues the text raises. These activities range from journal writing and prewriting exercises to classroom activities, such as debates and small group work, that encourage lively student involvement. We firmly believe that one of the best things a teacher can do is organize a class such that the students take charge of their own learning. Particularly in a writing class (but also in discipline-specific courses), students need to be active participants in their education. We've designed *Signs of Life* to allow students to do that. It is based on the premise that students come to college with a high level of expertise in popular culture that you can rely on to generate lively class discussion, inspire a commitment to learning, and create a community of writers within your class.

So what doesn't the manual do? It doesn't "give the answers" to the comprehension and writing/activity questions that follow each selection. We realize that some manuals take the instructor through answers step by step, but we haven't done that, for both practical and philosophical reasons. As is appropriate for a composition textbook, there are no readings here that you would have difficulty understanding, so we don't need to outline answers for the comprehension questions, although we do address cases where authors raise unusually thorny or problematic points. And even with comprehension questions, you may feel it appropriate for your students to emphasize one angle or another. The writing/activity questions don't have "right" or "wrong" responses, and they don't invite single correct answers. That's not to say that the questions are hard or that some responses might not be stronger than others. And we do provide suggestions for how you can use these questions with your students. It's just that we believe that critical thinking is nurtured if students explore an issue, sort out the evidence from several alternative sources that would best support a thesis, and consider what contrary positions might be held on an issue. In other words, the questions are intended to encourage students to *think* about an issue — to think thoroughly, specifically, and carefully. With that preparation, we believe, students are well on their way to becoming strong academic writers.

PREFACE

A word on the manual's organization is in order. We first provide an overview to using *Signs of Life* in your class, suggesting how to create thematic units, abbreviate chapters, or combine chapters, and giving hints on how to encourage student involvement. We also explain why we've used a semiotic approach and give you a little background history of semiotics. Next are two essays from instructors who have used *Signs of Life*, offering their advice to teachers new to the book. The bulk of the manual takes you through the readings, suggesting ways to use them in class and anticipating likely student reactions, creating links between selections and chapters, and providing hints on how you can have a lively discussion and assign successful writing topics based on the selections.

CONTENTS

Preface   iii

Using Popular Culture and Semiotics in the Composition Course   1
    Why Popular Culture?   1
    Why Semiotics?   1
    Some Background in Semiotics   2
    Responding to Questions about Semiotics   4
    Further Readings in Semiotics   6
Using *Signs of Life in the U.S.A.*   8
    The Text's Organization   8
    Alternative Thematic Arrangments   8
    Encouraging Student Response and Involvement   10
Advice from Experienced Instructors   14
Meredith Kurz, *Signs of Life in the Composition Class*   15
Deborah Banner, *Undergraduates in Grey Flannel Suits: Advertising in the Composition Classroom*   20

PART ONE: CULTURAL PRODUCTIONS   27

1. Consuming Passions: The Culture of American Consumption   27

Laurence Shames, *The More Factor*   29
Anne Norton, *The Signs of Shopping*   30
John de Graaf, David Wann, and Thomas H. Naylor, *The Addictive Virus*   30
Rachel Bowlby, *The Haunted Superstore*   31
Thomas Hine, *What's in a Package*   32
Fred Davis, *Blue Jeans*   33
Joan Kron, *The Semiotics of Home Decor*   33
David Goewey, *"Careful, You May Run Out of Planet": SUVs and the Exploitation of the American Myth*   34
Damien Cave, *The Spam Spoils of War*   35
Benjamin R. Barber, *Jihad vs. McWorld*   35
Thomas L. Friedman, *Revolution Is U.S.*   36

2. Brought to You B(u)y: The Signs of Advertising   38

Roland Marchand, *The Parable of the Democracy of Goods*   39
Jack Solomon, *Masters of Desire: The Culture of American Advertising*   40
Diane Barthel, *A Gentleman and a Consumer*   40
Eric Schlosser, *Kid Kustomers*   41
Gloria Steinem, *Sex, Lies, and Advertising*   42
James B. Twitchell, *What We Are to Advertisers*   43
John E. Calfee, *How Advertising Informs to Our Benefit*   44
Kalle Lasn, *Hype*   44
Portfolio of Advertisements   45

3. Video Dreams: Television, Music, and Cultural Forms   46

Todd Davis, The West Wing *in American Culture*   47
Steven D. Stark, The Oprah Winfrey Show *and the Talk-Show Furor*   48
Susan Douglas, *Signs of Intelligent Life on TV*   49

v

CONTENTS

Amanda Fazzone, *The Boob Tube*   49
Tad Friend, *You Can't Say That*   50
Tricia Rose, *Bad Sistas*   51
David Schiff, *The Tradition of the Oldie*   52
Robert Hilburn, *The Not-So-Big Hit Single*   53
Tom Shales, *Resisting the False Security of TV*   53
Marnie Carroll, *American Television in Europe*   54

4. The Hollywood Sign: The Culture of American Film   55

Robert B. Ray, *The Thematic Paradigm*   56
Linda Seger, *Creating the Myth*   57
Gary Johnson, *The Western*   57
Susan Bordo, *Braveheart, Babe, and the Contemporary Body*   58
Todd Boyd, *So You Wanna Be a Gangsta?*   59
Jessica Hagedorn, *Asian Women in Film: No Joy, No Luck*   60
Sandra Tsing Loh, *The Return of Doris Day*   60
Michael Parenti, *Class and Virtue*   61
Vivian C. Sobchack, *The Postmorbid Condition*   62
Patrick Goldstein, *The Time to Get Serious Has Come*   63

PART TWO: CULTURAL CONSTRUCTIONS   65

5. Popular Spaces: Interpreting the Built Environment   65

Malcolm Gladwell, *The Science of Shopping*   66
Anna McCarthy, *Brand Identity at NikeTown*   67
Susan Willis, *Disney World: Public Use/Private State*   68
Lucy R. Lippard, *Alternating Currents*   68
Karen Karbo, *The Dining Room*   69
Daphne Spain, *Spatial Segregation and Gender Stratification in the Workplace*   70
Rina Swentzell, *Conflicting Landscape Values: The Santa Clara Pueblo and Day School*   71
Camilo José Vergara, *The Ghetto Cityscape*   71
Eric Boehlert, *New York's Most Disliked Building?*   72

6. We've Come a Long Way, Maybe: Gender Codes in American Culture   74

Holly Devor, *Gender Role Behaviors and Attitudes*   75
Kevin Jennings, *American Dreams*   76
Deborah Blum, *The Gender Blur: Where Does Biology End and Society Take Over?*   77
Jennifer Scanlon, *Boys-R-Us: Board Games and the Socialization of Young Adolescent Girls*   78
Andre Meyer, *The New Sexual Stone Age*   78
Naomi Wolf, *The Beauty Myth*   79
Deborah Tannen, *There Is No Unmarked Woman*   80
James William Gibson, *Warrior Dreams*   80
Laura Miller, *Women and Children First: Gender and the Settling of the Electronic Frontier*   81

7. Constructing Race: Readings in Multicultural Semiotics   82

Michael Omi, *In Living Color: Race and American Culture*   83
Benjamin DeMott, *Put on a Happy Face: Masking the Differences between Blacks and Whites*   84

Paul C. Taylor, *Funky White Boys and Honorary Soul Sisters*   84
Jack Lopez, *Of Cholos and Surfers*   85
Nell Bernstein, *Goin' Gangsta, Choosin' Cholita*   86
bell hooks, *Baby*   86
Melissa Algranati, *Being an Other*   87
Fan Shen, *The Classroom and the Wider Culture: Identity as a Key
    to Learning English Composition*   87
LynNell Hancock, *The Haves and the Have-Nots*   88
Randall Kennedy, *Blind Spot*   89

8. It's Not Just a Game: Sports and American Culture   90

D. Stanley Eitzen, *The Contradictions of Big-Time College Sport*   91
Frank Deford, *Athletics 101: A Change in Eligibility Rules Is Long Overdue*   92
David Kamp, *America's Spaz-Time*   93
Michael A. Messner, *Power at Play: Sport and Gender Relations*   94
Mariah Burton Nelson, *I Won. I'm Sorry.*   94
Henry Jenkins, *"Never Trust a Snake": WWF Wrestling as Masculine Melodrama*   95
E. M. Swift and Don Yaeger, *Unnatural Selection*   96
Gary Smith, *The Boys on the Bus*   96

9. American Icons: The Mythic Characters of Popular Culture   97

Michael Eric Dyson, *Be Like Mike? Michael Jordan and the Pedagogy of Desire*   98
Gary Engle, *What Makes Superman So Darned American?*   99
Andy Medhurst, *Batman, Deviance, and Camp*   99
N'Gai Croal and Jane Hughes, *Lara Croft, the Bit Girl*   100
Emily Prager, *Our Barbies, Ourselves*   100
Gary Cross, *Barbie, G.I. Joe, and Play in the 1960s*   101
Mark Caldwell, *The Assault on Martha Stewart*   102
Roy Rivenburg, *Snap! Crackle! Plot!*   102
Jenny Lyn Bader, *Larger Than Life*   103
Tim Layden, *A Patriot's Tale*   103

USING POPULAR CULTURE AND SEMIOTICS IN THE COMPOSITION COURSE

Why Popular Culture?

We decided to focus this text on popular culture because we are convinced that students think and write at their best when they are in command of their subject matter. This is crucial when students are learning university-level writing strategies, for the newness of a subject can make students lack confidence as writers or lead them to adopt ineffective writing habits. Sometimes, for instance, students may oversummarize an issue because they are just learning about it and, essentially, are explaining it to themselves. *Signs of Life* is designed to take advantage of students' literacy in popular culture to generate sharp analysis and insightful interpretations. This is not to say that we assume all students are voracious consumers of popular culture in the same way. On the contrary: we assume that our readers will come to the book from a variety of backgrounds and with a variety of interests and experiences. The book, and particularly the apparatus, should allow students to share that variety through class and group activities.

In keeping with the increasing academic interest in cultural studies, we also assume an inclusive definition of popular culture. We address topics like advertising that traditionally have been considered part of popular culture, but we also include issues such as race that form part of America's social and cultural fabric. This notion of popular culture differs from the one that reigned when we began teaching twenty-five years ago. We recall a textbook that, as its nod to "popular culture," asked students to compare and contrast a Volkswagen and a Porsche, with no attention to the cars' social or cultural significance. This text used popular culture as an occasion for teaching rhetorical modes; in contrast, *Signs of Life* addresses the way broader issues, such as gender and ethnicity, affect cultural values and ideologies. As a result, we hope that your students will find the materials in *Signs of Life* to be both personally engaging and intellectually stimulating — among the two most important ingredients for a successful writing class.

In our experience, students respond to the materials in *Signs of Life* with delight, a little surprise, and great enthusiasm. Indeed, instructors who used the first three editions report that their students complete reading assignments and come to class eager to discuss and debate the issues. You'll find that your students often will be the experts on a subject, knowing more about, say, the latest band than you do. For some instructors that may be a discomforting role reversal. But we encourage you to let your students enjoy the role of expert, for that may well be their first step on the road to enjoying the role of writer.

Why Semiotics?

By making our choice of a semiotic approach explicit, we've departed from some textbook conventions. Traditionally, textbook authors assume a neutral stance toward their material, playing the role of objective compiler. Students then read the text, their task being to argue about or analyze it. But we see problems in this formulation of the roles of both author and student. As a comparison of textbooks can easily show, no textbook author is a mere compiler: the choices of what to include or exclude can reveal the author's values, philosophies, and ideologies. This point is hardly new (witness the many recent critiques of the canon), but our semiotic approach is designed to put this point into practice.

Discussed less often is the role of the student. It has long struck us that textbooks invite students to analyze, but textbooks authors hardly ever say what that means. There's the old "break up into constituent parts" definition, but that often remains a mystery to students: we're not even sure what it means when applied to real issues that don't have distinct parts. Essentially, analysis remains a pure category, with theoretical assumptions and ideological positions unexplored and undefined. But we don't believe there's such a thing as pure analysis, even for students. Indeed, it's likely that, in their discipline-specific courses, students will be asked to use various approaches or theories in their essays. In a sociology class, for instance, students may be asked to perform a Marxist analysis of a social problem; in an economics class, they may be assigned to assess tax-cutting proposals from a supply-side perspective. Being self-conscious about one's point of view is essential to academic writing; we can think of no better place for students to learn that lesson than in a writing class, and the semiotic approach is especially suited to this purpose.

Our own experience has borne this out. As an analytic method, semiotics teaches students to formulate cogent, well-supported interpretations. It emphasizes the examination of assumptions and beliefs and the way language shapes our apprehension of the world. Most students feel comfortable with semiotics: since one of its precepts is that its job is to *reveal* interests and ideologies, not to *judge* them, students are less likely to feel that you are peddling a single point of view on a topic if you adopt a semiotic approach. Semiotics also makes it easier for a class to discuss sensitive or politically charged issues: the goal is not to judge individuals' beliefs but to locate those beliefs within a social and cultural context.

Using semiotics in a writing class makes sense, too, because of things our students have told us. Much to our delight, students sometimes report that they're covering semiotics in another class. That shouldn't be too surprising, for semiotics also has the benefit of being a cross-disciplinary approach. A wing of critical theory in literature departments, semiotics also has been influential in film and media studies, anthropology, law, pyschology, sociology, political science, and even management studies. Although we can't guarantee that all students will revisit semiotics in their academic future, we feel its cross-disciplinary nature makes it suitable for a writing class made up of students who are studying a variety of majors and disciplines. Finally, our students have told us that they enjoy semiotics. In fact, we've had students say that they appreciate learning something entirely *new* in our classes, and what's new extends beyond the topics covered to a way of looking at the world.

With all that said, we recognize that a semiotics approach may be new to some instructors. We've accordingly designed the book to allow you to be as "semiotic" with your class as you choose. We'll be delighted if you discuss semiotics with your students, try out semiotic readings in class, and assign semiotic essay topics. But if you prefer to use the approach with a lighter touch, that's fine, too. Indeed, colleagues have told us that they appreciate the fact that the text does not obligate them to spend a lot of time with semiotics or to involve the class in technical definitions (we've avoided the technical jargon that makes much semiotics research seem turgid). Your class may be content knowing that semiotics means the interpretation of popular culture — and that can be your focus.

Some Background in Semiotics

Students often become intrigued by semiotics, asking about its history and wondering how they can learn about it. We'll anticipate their most common questions here, but don't worry, you don't have to be an expert to answer their questions. Their first question may well be: "Semi what? How do you pronounce it?" Well, it's simple: /semióktiks/. The word might seem unfamiliar because it was coined a little more than a century ago by Charles Sanders Peirce, who derived it from the Greek word for sign, or meaning — *semeiotikos*. The fact that Peirce, who founded the modern study of semiotics in the last third of the nineteenth century, could adopt an ancient Greek term so readily testifies to the long heritage of reading signs. From Plato and Aristotle to the Stoics, ancient philosophers speculated on the nature of signs; indeed, the Stoic philosophers anticipated contemporary semiotic theory by arguing that the meaning of a sign lies in a concept, not in a thing or referent.

Despite its antiquity, semiotics may be unfamiliar because unlike linguistics, which is a regular part of the university curriculum, relatively few colleges have programs or departments in semiotics. Most semiotic study takes place within disciplines such as literary and film studies and anthropology; here, the emphasis tends to be on semiotic theory — which, like any theoretical study, can be technical and forbidding. But just as you don't need to master transformational generative linguistics to decode a sentence, you don't need to master theoretical semiotics to perform semiotic analyses. In fact, we do just that every day, especially in regard to popular culture — and that's why students are perfectly capable of using a semiotic approach.

Students really need only a few basic principles to conduct a semiotic analysis. The first is that the meaning of a sign — whether it is a linguistic symbol, an artifact, a belief, or a form of behavior — is to be found within the system to which it belongs, not in some absolute realm of nature or reality. In semiotic terms, the meaning of a linguistic sign, for example, lies in its place within a system of culturally constituted concepts, not in a "real" object to which it refers. Similarly, in popular culture, a BMW gets its significance from its place in the system of automotive status symbols, not from its reference to any sort of concrete referent. It can at once be *associated* with other status symbols (like Land Rovers) and *differentiated* from non-status cars like Hyundais. Through such differential and associational relations, the meaning of a popular sign is constructed. Your students may want to insist that BMWs are popular because they're built well, that they refer to some objective measure of quality, but that functional answer fails to account for the many well-built cars that do not carry the status value of a "beamer." Just ask them to compare a BMW to an Oldsmobile. The difference between the two cars as they appear within the system is where the meaning lies, in the images that they project, not in the materials with which they are constructed. If your students doubt this, ask them to consider why Oldsmobile tried so hard to change its products' image among youthful consumers in its rather futile "This Is Not Your Father's Oldsmobile" campaign.

In technical terms, the systematic interpretation of a popular sign represents an adaptation of Ferdinand de Saussure's semiological principle that the meaning of a linguistic sign lies in its differences with respect to all the other signs in a linguistic system. Because structural semiology is a formalistic method that tends to ignore history and politics, we have expanded upon Saussure to add both Peircean and Marxist semiotic insights. From Peirce we take the principle that signs are situated in history and that their meanings shift as our knowledge or experience shifts. From Marxism we take the principle that cultural signs bear ideological weight. Thus, when we speak of the system to which a sign belongs, we refer to historical and ideological (or mythological) systems as well as formal ones. One could say that, in a broad sense, the semiotic method we propose resembles that found in Roland Barthes's *Mythologies*.

The ability to interpret something by locating it within an overall system is fundamental to any analytic writing, not just the interpretation of popular signs. As a result, teaching your students to see things like cars within their cultural contexts is a step toward helping them to see how, say, understanding Shakespeare in their literature classes requires a knowledge of the cultural system within which his plays appeared. The difference is that, with Shakespeare, the cultural system is historically alien to our time and must be learned. In our own time, the systems are well known; they simply need to be made explicit.

This should help you when, after interpreting the status value of something like a BMW, a student says, "Well, isn't all that obvious?" And, yes, semiotic analyses of popular culture sometimes may appear obvious, precisely because the systems within which popular signs appear are familiar. But ask your students if the meanings, say, of their clothing styles are obvious to their parents or to someone from a different culture who may have no knowledge of the fashion system to which American youth styles belong.

The key to teaching your students how to conduct semiotic analyses of popular culture is to cue them in to the social environments within which signs appear. In one sense, this involves the teaching of present history, which is rather different from the teaching of "current events." Current events tend to be the larger-than-life events — usually crises — that make headlines. Present history includes everything that we think and do on a day-to-day basis. Current events are macrofocused and have relatively little bearing on the conduct of our lives (unless we are in the center of them). Present history is microfocused, and part of semiotics is simply bringing to light the small things with which we live.

Thus, one need not be an expert in semiotic theory to be adept at semiotic interpretation. You may have studied semiotics in graduate school or as part of your postgraduate training, and though you may have found stimulating the writings of such semiotic masters as Ferdinand de Saussure, Charles Sanders Peirce, Roland Barthes, Umberto Eco, and Jean Baudrillard, you may still wonder how your composition students will fare in the realm of semiotics. You needn't worry. Just as one can write a syntactically flawless essay without knowing linguistic theory, one can go right to the heart of a cultural sign without bothering with whether Saussure or Peirce should be your guide. The secret is in the system, and that can be your focus.

Responding to Questions about Semiotics

The corollary to our fundamental semiotic precept, that the meaning of a sign is to be found in the system to which it belongs, is that meaning is a social construct, not a simple reflection of truth or reality. The systems within which our values and beliefs function are mythologies, not absolute revelations. This semiotic principle — that meaning is mythological (or ideological) in origin — may well raise the most challenging of your students' questions, questions that are likely to be of two sorts: scientific and moral. Here are some ways to cope with such questions.

Let's start with the scientific objections. We live in an empirical culture that believes in the truth of observation: If you want to get to the heart of something, all you need to do is look at it. European culture was not always like this, of course. In the Middle Ages, for example, the truths of faith were held to be higher than the truths of observation — so Galileo was ordered to retract what he said about what his telescope showed him. But since our society now believes in empirical observation, some students may be shaken by the semiotic suggestion that when we speak of "reality," and of the names we give to our experience of reality, we are speaking of the system of concepts within which we operate, a system that determines what it is possible for us to know.

For the semiotician, our knowledge reflects not ultimate realities but systems of values that can be called *worldviews* or *cultural myths*. Myths are not legends and stories in the semiotic view; they are value and belief systems that frame the very way we perceive and define reality. From a semiotic perspective, reality is not something waiting passively out there for us to discover: it is the product of our own interpretive decisions. There is always a semiotic frame, a mythology, that mediates between our consciousness and the reality we interpret, and therefore construct, because of that frame. This is one of the most profound, and disturbing, principles of semiotic understanding — disturbing because it flies in the face of our cultural belief in the sanctity of "objective" knowledge. For that reason, it is probably the most difficult obstacle to overcome in learning to think semiotically.

But a little history, read in the light of semiotic understanding, shows that our very belief in scientific objectivity is itself a form of interpretation, not an absolute fact. Fundamentally, your students will probably take a more or less positivistic approach if they object to semiotic principles. Positivism, a nineteenth-century philosophical movement that held that "truth" is revealed through the clear gaze of objective observation, is the ideology of most laypersons today when it comes to scientific interpretation. However, positivism is no longer in force among contemporary scientists. Modern scientists themselves take the position that the "truths" of science are fundamentally interpretations that are themselves made possible by what Thomas Kuhn, a scientific historian and philosopher, called the "paradigms" of "normal science." (Kuhn's book, *The Structure of Scientific Revolutions*, revolutionized the philosophy of science.) At any given time, according to Kuhn, a scientist pursues the research programs that the state of understanding at the moment permits. In an era of relativity, for example, physicists work within a relativistic paradigm of understanding. If relativity theory is ever overthrown, a new paradigm of understanding will emerge to govern future research. The object of study is reality, but it is the paradigm that determines what the researcher will look for and how it will be interpreted.

The profound effect our cultural mythologies have on the way we view reality can be seen by looking at the different ways that different cultures regard language itself. In European American culture, for example, the myth holds that the purpose of language is to communicate one's intentions, emotions, or meanings. Language, in short, is regarded as a transparent medium whose primary purpose is to convey information. The natural ground for language is considered to be logic and truth, the projection of objective facts, not persuasion and purpose. Thus, language is considered essentially apolitical, something that cannot ethically be manipulated. We even invent stories to support this mythology, taking America's most successful politician, George Washington, and glorifying him as an apolitical man who never told a lie. (Note how the myth stresses his reluctance when drafted as the first president.)

Things were not always thus in Western culture, however. In ancient Athens, wealthy men sent their sons to school primarily to learn the art of rhetoric, which was understood as the art of making political speeches. The Sophists, who ran the schools, specialized in rhetoric — teaching how to manipulate linguistic tropes to achieve one's ends. But it is not the Sophists whom we remember today (except negatively — the word *sophistical* now refers to an argument that can't be trusted). Rather, we remember Socrates, Plato's teacher, who hated the Sophists — among other things, he didn't like their habit of accepting tuition fees — and who believed that the purpose of language was to lead one objectively to absolute philosophical truth. Socrates' philosophical predilection to regard language logically and objectively eventually triumphed as the dominant language mythology of European culture. The Sophists' rhetorically based, political attitude toward language was defeated, and the philosophical view of language as an objective bearer of the truth became the now-invisible (because it is so widely embraced) linguistic myth of Western civilization.

Modern rhetoricians and semioticians, however, can point out just how many rhetorical tricks Plato used in his own writings to attack the rhetoricians of ancient Athens. (There is another irony here: Plato, the first great writer of secular prose in European history, despised and condemned writing as being too prone to trickiness and misinterpretation.) In other words, Western culture's embrace of an antirhetorical mythology of language is based, at least in part, upon some pretty fancy rhetoric. Plato, after all, got his way, which is what persuasive argumentation is meant to allow one to do.

Students may also raise a moral objection to semiotics; the approach can raise the specter of relativism. We think it is fair for students to ask, "If semiotics argues that values are culturally relative, then what's the point in having values?" Since such questions are difficult to answer, they may be either ignored or dismissed in a manner that suggests that some semioticians are eager enough to expose the ideological underpinnings of their opponents' values but that they consider their own values unassailable. We do not believe that this is a good way to teach semiotic thinking, so we will address the issue of ethical relativism that semiotics raises in a more tentative way. We intend to open up the question for further debate — perhaps the first debate you may engage in with your class.

Our first response to the "What's the point, then?" question is that every attempt to come up with an absolute standard of values is going to run into trouble anyway. Most commonly, people rely on religious teachings to provide moral guidance, but it doesn't take long to see how ambiguous things can get even when we can agree on the same guide. American moral culture, for example, is founded on the injunctions of the Bible, whose commandment on killing seems clear enough. "Thou shalt not kill," the commandment says, but then the interpretation begins. Killing nonhumans is rarely included in the injunction (though in Buddhist culture, the ideal is to kill no animal at all), but what about war, capital punishment, euthanasia, and that most intractable of controversies, abortion? If your students begin to pronounce judgment on such matters, let the class discussion reveal the sources of their judgments. Likely as not there will be disagreement, and when students probe the ground for their opinions, they will discover that many such grounds are possible. Ask your class, then, who gets to decide which ground is paramount, and the ensuing discussion should reveal just how political our values are.

The point, then, is not whether value systems are possible; it is how convincing we can be when presenting our values. Often, the mere challenge to justify one's opinions can illuminate their ideological foundations. Semiotic thinking teaches us to probe our values, not to give them up, and such probing can help us — especially as writers — find better ways of persuading others to adopt our point of view. Simply denouncing the opposition gets one nowhere: a writer has to find the terms that make most sense to a reader who may not share his or her perspective at first. Indeed, as semioticians, we have written this text with the understanding that the semiotic point of view is hardly universal but that if it is thoughtfully, even considerately, presented, it can contribute to anyone's intellectual growth.

Further Readings in Semiotics

If you want to pursue semiotics further, we suggest the following books as a place to start. Some are introductions to the field (and would also be suitable for student readers), while others are technical and theoretical.

Barthes, Roland. *The Fashion System.* Berkeley: Univ. of California Press, 1990. A classic semiotic reading of clothing styles.

———. *Mythologies*, trans. Annette Lavers. New York: Hill and Wang, 1972. One of the first applications of semiotic theory to the interpretation of popular culture. Barthes's wide-ranging analyses take in everything from the cultural significance of plastic and strip tease to professional wrestling and Einstein's brain.

Baudrillard, Jean. *America*. London: Verso, 1988. A classic reading of American culture, focusing on New York and Los Angeles, by the world's preeminent postmodern semiologist.

Berger, Asa. *Signs in Contemporary Culture: An Introduction to Semiotics*. New York: Longman, 1984. A popular introduction to semiotics, applying semiotic insights to the interpretation of Shakespeare, Sherlock Holmes, pop art, the comics, digital watches, baseball, and much more.

———. *Cultural Criticism: A Primer of Key Concepts*. Thousand Oaks, CA: Sage, 1995.

Blonsky, Marshall. *American Mythologies*. New York: Oxford, 1992. A reading of American popular culture.

———. *On Signs*. Baltimore: Johns Hopkins Univ. Press, 1985. An anthology of essays written by leading semioticians from Umberto Eco to Jacques Derrida. Essays range from technical expositions on semiotic theory to cultural and literary criticism.

Bondanella, Peter. *Umberto Eco and the Open Text: Semiotics, Fiction, Popular Culture*. Cambridge: Cambridge Univ. Press, 1997.

Clarke, D.S., Jr. *Sources of Semiotic: Readings With Commentary from Antiquity to the Present*. Carbondale: Southern Illinois Univ. Press, 1990. An anthology of semiotic writings from Aristotle to the present, with each selection annotated by Clarke.

Deely, John. *Basics of Semiotics*. Bloomington: Indiana Univ. Press, 1990. A primer in semiotic theory from one of the major figures in the Semiotic Society of America.

Eco, Umberto. *A Theory of Semiotics*. Bloomington: Indiana Univ. Press, 1979. A magisterial summation of semiotic theory from the world's leading semiotician, establishing a theoretical grounding for the connection between signs and culture.

———. *Travels in Hyperreality*. New York: Harcourt, Brace, 1990. A collection of essays that interpret American and Italian popular culture.

Hawkes, Terence. *Structuralism and Semiotics*. Berkeley: Univ. of California Press, 1977. A primer in structural semiology and deconstruction written for students of literary criticism and theory.

Hodge, Bob. *Social Semiotics*. Cambridge: Polity Press with Basil Blackwell, 1988.

Holbrook, Morris B., and Elizabeth C. Hirshman. *The Semiotics of Consumption*. New York: Mouton de Gruyter, 1993.

Nöth, Winfried. *Handbook of Semiotics*. Bloomington: Indiana Univ. Press, 1989. An encyclopedic dictionary of major semiotic terms and concepts.

Peirce, Charles Sanders. *Collected Papers*. 8 vols. Ed. Charles Hartshorne and Paul Weiss. Cambridge: Cambridge Univ. Press, 1931–66. Eight volumes of the original essays, papers, and random jottings that inaugurated the modern study of semiotics in America.

Saussure, Ferdinand de. *Course in General Linguistics*. Ed. Charles Bally and Albert Sechehage. Trans. Roy Harris. London: Duckworth, 1983. A transcription of the pioneering lectures that led to the development of semiology and structuralism.

Scholes, Robert. *Semiotics and Interpretation*. New Haven: Yale Univ. Press, 1982. An introduction to semiotics for students of literary theory and criticism.

Sebeok, Thomas, ed. *Encyclopedic Dictionary of Semiotics*. Berlin and New York: Mouton de Gruyter, 1986. A guide to semiotic terms and concepts, edited by the dean of American semiotics and the founder of the Semiotic Society of America.

Sebeok, Thomas, and Smith, Iris. *American Signatures: Semiotic Inquiry and Method*. Norman: Univ. of Oklahoma Press Project for Discourse and Theory, 1990. A collection of essays on problems in semiotics, including a historical overview of the growth of the semiotic enterprise in the United States.

Silverman, Kaja. *The Subject of Semiotics.* New York: Oxford Univ. Press, 1983. A psychoanalytic and feminist approach to semiotics, especially applied to films.

Solomon, Jack. *The Signs of Our Times: The Secret Meanings of Everyday Life.* New York: Harper/Collins Perennial Library, 1990. A nonacademic introduction to semiotics, focusing on its application to popular culture. Essays range from interpretations of TV shows and advertisements to toys, food, clothing, architecture, and postmodernism. This book has been used as a class text for college writing classes across the nation.

Umiker-Sebeok, Jean, ed. *Marketing and Semiotics: New Directions in the Study of Signs for Sale.* Berlin: Mouton de Gruyter, 1987. A collection of papers devoted to the semiotics of marketing goods and services.

Wollen, Peter. *Signs and Meaning in the Cinema.* Bloomington: Indiana Univ. Press, 1972. A semiotic approach to the interpretation of films.

Using *Signs of Life in the U.S.A.*

THE TEXT'S ORGANIZATION

We have divided *Signs of Life* into two major sections, both to enhance the text's flexibility and to highlight the essential cultural connection between the things we consume and the things we believe. Part One, Cultural Productions, focuses on the marketing and consumption of cultural products, particularly the objects we buy, the ads that sell us those objects, and the TV shows, videos, and films that shape and express our consuming passions. Your students will take to such topics immediately — they form the core of their cultural literacy — and your class ought to have a lot of fun with your assignments. Part Two, Cultural Constructions, may seem more sobering, but the issues presented there should be just as familiar to your students as are those of Part One. This half of the book encourages students to see that popular culture is a serious thing, shaped by beliefs and values that are often ignored when one considers only the gaudy imagery of the culture industry. Is *Pretty Woman* your students' favorite movie? Well, Chapter Six, on gender, can help them see the social undercurrents that made the film such a hit. Do some wonder why they feel out of place in an office environment, while others thrive in that setting? Both groups can connect with Chapter Five, "Popular Spaces: Interpreting the Built Environment." In short, behind every cultural production is ideology. What we do, whether at work at or play, is linked to what we believe, and the twofold division of *Signs of Life* is intended to emphasize graphically and thematically this fundamental semiotic connection.

ALTERNATIVE THEMATIC ARRANGEMENTS

You're not likely to march through *Signs of Life* chapter by chapter, assigning your students every selection; even if you want to do that, you probably wouldn't have time. You'll probably need to abbreviate the text to accommodate the length of your school term and the skill level of your students. There are better and worse ways to do that. One way, of course, is by covering the entire text but eliminating readings from each chapter. We advise against that simply because your students may feel frustrated by what can seem a whirlwind tour of topics (the "if it's Tuesday, it must be gender" feeling). Some instructors might choose to cover just one half of the book. Although that's a workable approach that would score points for focus, we'd be sorry to have students lose the deliberate cross-pollination of issues that occurs throughout the text. Here's a brief example. The images perpetuated by the media (Part One) are shaped by our culture's assumptions about race (Chapter Seven); similarly, prevailing beliefs about gender (Chapter Six) are reinforced and given legitimacy through advertising (Chapter Two), television (Chapter Three), and film (Chapter Four). If you emphasize just one half of the book, we urge you to include in your syllabus at least one chapter from the other half.

So what do we recommend? We strongly suggest beginning with the general introduction so that students can gain an overview of the book, understand the semiotic approach, and learn why they're covering popular culture in their writing class. At this point, you might ask them for their ideas on which selections they'd like to cover. Although it may seem scary to begin the course without everything mapped out in detail, you may win greater class involvement if you allow your students some say in what they have to read. Together you could pick and choose among all the selections, creating your own themes as you go along. As an alternative, you could plan out the first half of the course, then solicit student suggestions for what to cover during the second half. If you prefer more structure, we see two possible approaches: (1) organizing your course around one broad theme or (2) creating several small units, each with its own theme.

1. *Organizing your course around one broad theme.* Three of the chapters — "Consuming Passions: The Culture of American Consumption" (Chapter One), "We've Come a Long Way, Maybe: Gender Codes in American Culture" (Chapter Six), and "Constructing Race: Readings in Multicultural Semiotics" (Chapter Seven) — address themes far-ranging enough that you could select one and focus your entire course on the single theme it introduces. After beginning with one of these chapters and covering it entirely, you could pick among other chapters that contain readings related to the theme and select those that would most usefully enhance your approach to the overall topic. The following possibilities would work if you plan to cover five additional chapters, although you certainly can adapt these schemes or invent your own.

> *Theme:* Consuming Behavior in America
> Begin with: "Consuming Passions" (Chapter One)
> Do: "Brought to You B(u)y" (Chapter Two)
> Pick three: "Video Dreams" (Chapter Three), "The Hollywood Sign" (Chapter Four), "Popular Spaces" (Chapter Five), "We've Come a Long Way, Maybe" (Chapter Six), "American Icons" (Chapter Nine)
>
> *Theme:* Multiculturalism/Ethnicity
> Begin with: "Constructing Race" (Chapter Seven)
> Pick four: "Brought to You B(u)y" (Chapter Two), "Video Dreams" (Chapter Three), "The Hollywood Sign" (Chapter Four), "We've Come a Long Way, Maybe" (Chapter Six), "American Icons" (Chapter Nine)
>
> *Theme:* Gender
> Begin with: "We've Come a Long Way, Maybe" (Chapter Six)
> Pick four: "Brought to You B(u)y" (Chapter Two), "Video Dreams" (Chapter Three), "The Hollywood Sign" (Chapter Four), "Popular Spaces" (Chapter Five), "American Icons" (Chapter Nine)

2. *Creating several small units, each with its own theme.* Because the selections cover many interrelated themes, you could organize your course around several smaller issues. You'll probably spot such units as you skim through the book; we suggest some here that we find especially appealing. We also suggest possible readings from throughout the book, but by no means should this be read as a definitive list, nor should you feel obligated to cover all the readings suggested for each theme.

Ethnicity
Do: "Constructing Race" (Chapter Seven)
Pick from: Rose (Chapter Three); Boyd, Hagedorn, Loh (Chapter Four); Swentzell (Chapter Five); Eitzen (Chapter Eight); Dyson (Chapter Nine)

Consumerism/Commodification
Do: "Consuming Passions" (Chapter One)
Pick from: Marchand, Solomon, Schlosser, Steinem, Twitchell (Chapter Two); Hilburn (Chapter Three); Gladwell, McCarthy, Willis (Chapter Five); Omi, Hancock (Chapter Seven); Dyson, Prager, Cross, Caldwell, Rivenburg (Chapter Nine)

Gender
Do: "We've Come a Long Way, Maybe" (Chapter Six)
Pick from: Bowlby (Chapter One); Barthel, Steinem (Chapter Two); Stark, Douglas, Fazzone, Rose (Chapter Three); Bordo, Hagedorn, Loh, Sobchack (Chapter Four); Lippard, Karbo, Spain (Chapter Five); Messner, Nelson, Jenkins (Chapter Eight); Medhurst, Croal and Hughes, Prager, Cross (Chapter Nine)

The Formation of Personal Identity
Begin with Kron (Chapter One)
Pick from: de Graaf et al., Hine, Davis, Goewey (Chapter One); Twitchell (Chapter Two); Bordo (Chapter Four); Devor, Jennings, Blum, Scanlon, Wolf, Gibson (Chapter Six); Lopez, Bernstein, Algranati, Shen (Chapter Seven); Messner, Nelson (Chapter Eight); Bader (Chapter Nine)

Interpreting Signs and Images
Do: "American Icons" (Chapter Nine); cover, frontispieces, images, and photos throughout the text
Pick from: Norton, Hine, Davis, Kron, Goewey (Chapter One); Solomon, Barthel, Portfolio of Ads (Chapter Two); Davis, Stark, Douglas (Chapter Three); Bordo, Boyd, Hagedorn, Loh, Parenti (Chapter Four); Willis, Karbo, Vergara, Boehlert (Chapter Five); Devor, Scanlon, Mayer, Wolf, Tannen, Gibson (Chapter Six); Omi, Bernstein, hooks, Kennedy (Chapter Seven); Kamp, Nelson (Chapter Eight)

Cultural Implications of the September 11, 2001, Terrorist Attacks
Do: September 11 Portfolio
Pick from: Cave, Barber, Friedman (Chapter One); Shales (Chapter Three); Goldstein (Chapter Four); Boehlert (Chapter Five); Kennedy (Chapter Seven); Smith (Chapter Eight); Layden (Chapter Nine)

Encouraging Student Response and Involvement

Signs of Life presumes a class with active students. It calls on their knowledge of popular culture and encourages them to participate in their writing class. We've built into the apparatus suggestions for a variety of ways students can respond to readings, reflect on them alone, and discuss them with others. We've tried to suggest responses that are appropriate to each reading. For instance, we include at least one reflective journal topic for selections that might disturb readers. But our suggestions are meant to be flexible: that we frame a topic as an essay question, for instance, doesn't mean that you can't rewrite it as a journal prompt. We'll summarize for you the major strategies we've relied on to trigger students' response, and we'll offer whatever hints we can for ensuring their success.

Cover On the first day of class, you might start by asking students to interpret the cover. What's the significance of the Rubik's cube? What does its inclusion suggest about the text's approach to popular culture? And ask your students to study the images on the cube as well. How do they function as signs of American culture? Should there be any dispute about what the images are, here's a quick run-down. The top panel: the Statue of Liberty, hamburger, stop sign, laptop, ice cream cone, shopping cart, dustbroom and pan, "sale" sign, U.S. flag. The left panel: handgun, cell phone, outlet, White House, bar code, soccer ball, basketball, mailbox, cloudy earth. The right panel: earth as a map, jeans, computer circuits, coffee cup, firefighter ladder, baseball, airplane, hotdog, computer keyboard.

Frontispieces and Images We feel that it's essential for a semiotics-based reader to include both images and text, so each chapter begins with a frontispiece that presents an image related to the chapter's topic, and throughout the book appear photos and images ripe for analysis. Do discuss these images with your students, perhaps as a way to begin class discussion of a new topic. Some, such as the Calvin and Hobbes frontispiece (Chapter Three), offer critical commentary of their own. Some illustrate points mentioned in the chapter introductions or articles (the frontispiece showing the Eaton Centre Mall, for instance, demonstrates the discussion in Chapter Five's introduction). Others coordinate with adjacent articles (the photograph of Salt 'N' Pepa meshes with the Rose selection in Chapter Three, for instance, just as the photo of Serena Williams accompanies the Nelson piece in Chapter Eight). Some extend the issues raised in adjacent articles (such as the babies in the cart in Chapter Six). Discuss with your students both the immediate impact the images have on them — their gut reponses — and the images' cultural and social significance. To get your students thinking about an issue, ask them to brainstorm alternative images and then to debate which ones they would or would not want to see in a text. Not only would such a discussion reveal much about their own worldview, it would enable students to see that they've already been semioticians all along.

In addition, we've included a Portfolio of September 11 photographs. Not only does it serve as a memorial to those who lost their lives and a recognition of those who struggled to save the victims; in addition, we include it as a reminder of the enormity of the events of that terrible day. The September 11 attacks have been compared to other landmark historical moments — Pearl Harbor, the assassination of John F. Kennedy — that have altered the course of American history and culture. Ask your students about their responses to watching images of the attacks as they happened. How do they compare the responses they had then with those they have today? In what way do the events of September 11 serve as a defining moment of their generation?

Introduction We consider the general introduction essential if you plan to use the semiotic approach, for that's where we not only explain the method and our rationale for using it but also walk students through sample interpretations that can serve as models for their own analyses. Notice that often we stop short of completing an analysis. We've deliberately not provided definitive readings of the topics raised; instead, we try to give just enough so that students will be excited and encouraged to pursue their own interpretations. Thus, often we stop in the middle of an analysis and turn to the students. Use such moments as a way to stimulate class discussion. Ask your students to finish the job — to amplify and extend, or even to contradict, the analyses that we've started. Even if you don't use semiotics, the introduction explains why their textbook focuses on popular culture as its topic.

Writing about Popular Culture We recognize that many students, even early in their writing process, may want to see what a "real" essay looks like as a model to guide their own revision and thinking. We've thus included in our introduction suggestions for writing on popular culture as well as student-written essays on topics prompted by this text. Of course, you may wish to supplement this material with sample essays written by your own students. But these sample essays are particularly useful if you want to review student work early in the term before your own students have produced any final drafts, or you may prefer the diplomatically easier choice of critiquing an essay not written by someone sitting in class.

This section has two parts: an introduction to writing about popular culture and three sample students essays. You can assign the introductory comments with or without the subsequent essays — the two can exist independently if you like. The introductory material would be best assigned early in the term, perhaps even before students start their first writing assignment. Here we emphasize prewriting strategies, especially invention techniques, and offer suggestions for writing arguments about popular culture. Specifically, we emphasize constructing a strong argument with specific evidence — one of the most common need of students, even at varying levels and abilities, is to learn how to translate their personal reactions and private opinions into a defensible argument that can stand up in the court of public discussion. Our comments are intended not to be exhaustive but rather to suggest to your students how academic discourse demands that writers be responsible to their readership, in addition to their own ideas.

The second part presents three student essays, chosen because they represent a range of styles and topics, with brief marginal annotations. Although we believe each writer is effective in achieving his or her goals, be aware that, as with any student writing, there's always room for improvement. So we suggest that you describe these essays not as "ideal" models — that might intimidate some students, anyway — but as interesting and effective responses to some of the issues *Signs of Life* raises. If your students can suggest revisions to strengthen the essays, great!

The first essay, by William Martin-Doyle of Harvard University, is a strong semiotic reading of *Cool Hand Luke*. This essay is particularly useful if you're emphasizing text-based arguments, as Martin-Doyle draws on Robert B. Ray's "The Thematic Paradigm" in Chapter Four for his critical framework. Interestingly, Martin-Doyle departs from Ray in his argument, showing a spirit of intellectual independence that we think is worth promoting. In addition, the argument is supported with a good, close reading of the film. We recognize that some students may not have seen *Cool Hand Luke*. That shouldn't be a problem, because students can focus on how Martin-Doyle draws on both Ray's essay and the film to construct his own interpretation. If curious, students can rent the video (or you may wish to do that yourself).

The second essay, by Dana Mariano of Lehigh University, is based on her experience with a recent popular trend: tattooing and body piercing. This is a fully accessible essay that we selected because Mariano goes beyond simply narrating her visit to the tattoo parlor to interpret the appeal of the fad itself — a nice blend of the personal and the broader social context. We include the third essay, by Mike Nordberg of Lehigh University, because students often receive open-ended assignments but don't quite know where to go with them. Mike's essay provides a good model of how to focus a topic and how to ground it in lots of specific, relevent details.

Chapter Introductions and Boxed Questions A crucial part of the book, the chapter introductions suggest ways to analyze the chapter's subject and provide a critical framework for reading and understanding the essays that follow. Such a framework is vital for a popular-culture textbook, for the students' strengths can become their weaknesses. Because students know so much about the culture around them, it's sometimes hard for them to adopt a critical stance toward it; guiding students toward that critical stance is one of the introductions' main tasks. The introductions suggest ways to read a subject, model interpretations of examples, link the various issues raised by the selections, and (as with the general introduction) create opportunities for students to explore an issue further. You can also trigger discussion by assigning the boxed questions included with each introduction. "The Exploring the Signs" questions are all journal or prewriting topics, intended to stimulate a student's thinking on a topic even before you discuss it in class. Most relate the chapter's subject to the student's personal experience, and they're meant to lead students to see how a broad or abstract topic can apply to their own lives. The "Discussing the Signs" boxes suggest in-class activities such as debates, discussions, or small-group work. You could try these tasks either on the day you discuss the chapter introduction or any time when you're covering the chapter readings. The "Reading on the Net" exercises suggest ways to investigate a topic on the Internet. Some Net exercises send students online to research a topic, while others ask them to interpret what they find at a given Web site. In some cases, we've given specific Internet addresses, but be aware that the Net is always changing — your students may find alternative sites that are as interesting as the ones we've suggested.

"Reading the Text" Questions All selections are accompanied first by questions we've dubbed "Reading the Text," essentially comprehension questions designed to ensure careful, accurate reading. They ask students to identify the selections' key concepts, to explain difficult terms, and to articulate how the selections' main ideas relate to each other and to the evidence the authors present. These questions are ideal for readings logs or journals. You could routinely assign them whenever you give a reading assignment, or you could assign them just for selections you anticipate may be difficult for your students. We suggest that you create some mechanism whereby your students can share their responses with others. You might begin discussion of a reading by asking some students to read their responses to the class; that will enable you to see quickly whether your students had any trouble understanding the selection. Alternatively, your students could share their responses in small groups, or they might write brief responses on the board at the beginning of class.

"Reading the Signs" Questions Each selection is also accompanied by various writing and activity questions designed to produce clear analytic thinking and strong student writing. You'll see that most "Reading the Signs" questions call for a written response to the text. Some we've framed as journal topics; we find it valuable pedagogically for students to be able to link the sometimes abstract or theoretical concepts to their own lives. Seeing that their schoolwork doesn't have to exist independently of their home culture can prove a tremendous motivation for students. Journal entries can also be particularly useful for selections that might disturb your students; writing in their journals allows them a chance to explore their responses before they get to class. Occasionally, you might ask students to read their entries aloud in small groups or before the entire class (for sensitive topics, you might read the entries to the class yourself, without revealing the students' names). But be sure to let your class know at the beginning of the term whether the journal is to be public (shared with other students) or private (shared with just you), or both.

The essay questions range from fairly simple and straightforward to challenging and controversial, calling for different modes of response (argumentation, comparison, and so forth). Some topics focus on a single selection, while others ask students to consider two or more selections in relation to each other. You'll find that some questions ask students to conduct nontraditional research, such as interviews. We've found that students become excited when doing such work and that they often produce their best writing when they can generate their own primary evidence. To ensure successful interviews, you should provide them with some guidelines ahead of time. You might discuss with your class the difference between questions that are open-ended and those that prompt yes-no responses. You could ask students to prepare interview questions for your review. Particularly if students will be asking about sensitive topics, they can benefit from role-playing an interview in small groups. Role-playing can also help students with timing; they usually underestimate how long it will take to cover a set of issues.

A number of questions invite other in-class activities, such as group work, debates, and hypothetical conversations. We encourage you to try these to stimulate all your students to participate. We've found small groups can work for almost any sort of class activity, from discussing a selection to writing a collaborative research paper. Small groups often allow students to be more honest, and being in a group can make it easier for quiet students to participate in the class. We particularly like to use groups to create a different class dynamic than exists during a whole-class discussion. In addressing gender issues, for instance, you can create same-sex groups to discuss an issue and then have the groups report to the whole class. That way not only will students benefit from their group discussion, but they can stand back and examine the groups themselves for evidence of gender-based patterns. One kind of group work that can yield surprising results is a hypothetical conversation between two authors or characters from the readings. We like these conversations because students must first discuss among themselves the likely positions each author would take on an issue (*what* the author would say); then they must consider the manner of presentation appropriate for each author (*how* the author would say it). If you ask your students to stage such a conversation, be sure to give them plenty of time for planning it — that's when half the learning takes place!

Debates are particularly valuable for teaching argumentative strategies: students must generate logical arguments, amass compelling evidence, and anticipate opposing viewpoints. When creating debating teams, we've found it works best to mix students of various viewpoints — in other words, it's not necessary for everyone on a team to hold the same opinion of an issue. If the group members have different opinions, students will be exposed to alternative positions when planning their presentations.

Some questions call for nonanalytic assignments, such as designing an advertisement. Do give these a try; they provide students with a chance to put the analytical and theoretical material to practical use. Students may see such assignments as just fun, so we suggest that you create some mechanism whereby they reflect on or analyze their creations. They might present their work to the class, explaining the rationale behind it; or, in an essay, they could describe their goals and discuss the extent to which their creation fulfilled those goals.

Glossary of Key Terms   We include a glossary of key words and concepts drawn from the chapter introductions to provide a ready reference for you and your students.

Citing Sources   On the end pages appears a brief guide to citing sources, including on-line and media sources, for your students' quick reference.

Companion Web Site   For supplementary material, consult the Web site that accompanies this text at **www.bedfordstmartins.com/signsoflife**. This Web site offers a rich array of links, from manufacturers' sites that are ripe for analysis and interpretation to critical sites, such as one for Ken Burns's PBS documentary *The West*, to archives such as the American Advertising Museum. You can search our companion Web site either by chapter or by subject.

Advice from Experienced Instructors

Since we began working on the first edition of *Signs of Life* several years ago, we have benefited from the fresh ideas and innovative teaching techniques of our friends and colleagues. For this version of the instructor's manual, we thought we should share some of this helpful advice with you. Meredith Kurz of California State University, Northridge, provides suggestions for an array of pedagogical issues, ranging from sequencing assignments throughout the term to preventing plagiarism. Next, Deborah Banner of UCLA describes an imaginative class project that involves group work, student presentations, the collaborative creation of an ad, and individual student essays. We find their ideas striking and believe you will as well, whether you're new to *Signs of Life* or a veteran.

MEREDITH KURZ
SIGNS OF LIFE IN THE COMPOSITION CLASS

My title's obviously pilfered wordplay echoes what I believe to be the spirit of this textbook and its perhaps secondary or tertiary message — that a somewhat less than deadly serious approach to the subject of composition and composition pedagogy is not undesirable. When all is said and done, to write is to play, and to teach writing also is to play — to play with ideas, writing techniques, grammar, and words. The problem I faced in teaching my early semesters was that I had not yet found my own way to that realization; consequently, there was no way that I could help my students find their own way there. But since lately I have made some modest progress in that respect, I submit my roadmap for perusal by both novice and seasoned instructors. It is marked with concepts, directions, tips, and other miscellanea that I have picked up along the way from professorial mentors, collegial colleagues, and anyone else who had something to offer and did.

During the first of my university's two teaching assistant training semesters, my composition director gave our class some very useful advice: "Get a good textbook, and let it support you," she said. With this idea in mind, we TAs set about finding the most supportive book available and chose for our first-teaching-semester textbook a reader-rhetoric-handbook combination. We were motivated to select such a text for three reasons:

- For our students' sakes (having everything included in one book would lower course costs for them);
- By our own insecurities (this textbook was so complete that it could teach the course all by itself; then we would be able to relax and cruise right through our first semester because "we had a good textbook, and we were going to let it support us"); and
- Because our instructor advised us to choose that particular textbook.

That first semester, I cleaved to that book with religious fervor, presenting the text to my students, chapter and verse, rigidly following the order of the textbook from Chapter One and forward. Then, somewhere around midsemester, I realized that I was losing my class's interest and my own energy. My undeviating progress through the textbook was boring me to death, and I seemed to be taking my students with me. Certainly, none of us was turning out any deathless prose. This complete textbook dependence on my part fostered a rigidity that worked to stifle almost all the original ideas anyone might have had, to abort any innovative writing styles that may have been gestating in my students' minds, and to suffocate whatever creative teaching I might have attempted.

Fortunately, at about that time, my composition director gave our TA class (many of whom found themselves in a similar situation) a second very useful bit of advice: "Don't allow your textbook to control you," she said. At first, this new useful advice seemed to contradict the old useful advice, until I realized that support and control are two entirely different concepts. At that point, I decided to change to a less prescriptive textbook format so that I wouldn't be tempted to lean so heavily on it. Accordingly, I set about finding a book that would afford my students and me a greater degree of flexibility, offer some not unwanted guidance, and yet not encourage dependence. Please forgive me if I sound like a textbook commercial here, but it was just about then that *Signs of Life in the U.S.A.* (hereinafter affectionately referred to as *SOL*) came into my life — just in time to breathe some life into my teaching. A reader with something extra, *SOL* provided both the readings and the "way" for my class and for me. *SOL* is a textbook that offers instructive but not pedantic readings and that provides a flexible and dynamic analytical methodology for reading and for writing. Additionally, the sheer number and diversity of essays make the textbook adaptable to many different types of semester formats, allowing room for instructor creativity and providing enough material for a multitude of assignment focuses.

I also welcomed the move from division by modes — to my mind, a rather outmoded and useless structure — to this text's focus on popular culture, semiotic methodology, and subject-oriented organization. The textbook's content, approach, and arrangement are such that anyone from anywhere can find material of interest and a way to write about it. Equally important, however, I also found in *SOL* room to play and flexible rules to play by. Although it may have been too late to resurrect my first semester, I had found a way to infuse life into my second.

Here ends the testimonial for *SOL* and begins some (I hope) useful suggestions for its application.

My Choice: The Assignment-Driven Semester

Some colleges and universities supply to their composition faculty a departmentally mandated textbook and require that the composition course follow its, usually, prescriptive text. I have been fortunate enough never to have worked in such circumstances except in my first TA semester. The English departments for which I have taught generally have given me a wide choice of textbooks as well as the discretion to formulate my semester as I see fit. Each has supplied me with only a very general course outline that allows for a great deal of creativity on my part. These course outlines vary little from school to school and seem to adhere to the following broad assignment pattern: (1) the narrative essay, (2) the analysis essay, (3) the argument essay, and (4) the research essay. Making semester planning a bit more complex, at California State University, Northridge, where I did my TA training and teaching, the department required, in addition to the class textbook, a full-text nonfiction work as well.

My first semester's semidisaster served me well in helping me to devise my second. I learned a lot from that experience, and one important lesson involved that first essay assignment — the narrative. In that first semester, most students turned in narratives that were exclusive rather than inclusive. These essays could not have been of interest to anyone but the writer herself and maybe, just maybe, her best friend. The writing was far too personal and, unfortunately, set a tone for the semester that I found difficult to dislodge. Subsequent essays, no matter what their purpose, always seemed to emerge from a too-personal point of view and consequently spoke only to an exclusive audience, no matter what purpose and audience directives I had supplied. I realized that the problem had a great deal to do with the students' rhetorical maturity and that it was my job to move them from their writing adolescence into a writing adulthood. Clearly, I needed to set up a model that would move them from "I" to "we" and finally to "they" — from subjective to intersubjective to objective, the academic objective being the writing style that they needed to acquire. My goal would be to achieve a synthesis between the four types of essays required and the three rhetorical stances I wished to move them through.

My Unit I: Narrative (The Inclusive "I")

My whole text, Mike Rose's excellent autobiographical narrative *Lives on the Boundary* (New York: Penguin, 1990), provided a perfect jumping off point for the semester. Rose writes an autobiographical narrative that is "I" oriented but also discusses many other issues, literacy among them, and literacy, after all, is what we are after in our classes. After two weeks spent reading, discussing, and writing about the Rose narrative, it was an easy segue into *SOL*, where I began by assigning a personal literacy narrative. Fan Shen's "The Classroom and the Wider Culture: Identity as a Key to Learning English Composition" (Chapter Seven) chronicles the author's rhetorical journey from his own culture's composition form to our Western academic approach. In so doing, he explores the differences in form and style and the cultural and ideological reasons behind those differences. Most freshman composition students have no idea that writing form and style varies from culture to culture, so interacting with Shen's essay is a real eye opener for them. From studying Shen's "I" (more than just personal) narratives, the students glean new and interesting information and perspectives from content and at the same time gain a more sophisticated understanding of personal narrative form. They learn that each of them can universalize the "I" and that their "I" can signify something beyond themselves. With this preparation, the students attempted their first essay, the "I" narrative. The assignment asked them to write either a cultural autobiography, a cultural biography, or a literacy narrative and, like the authors of their textbook models, to write inclusively rather than exclusively.

My Unit II: Analysis (The Cultural "We")

In the second unit, students moved from a subjective to an intersubjective point of view, focusing on how we construct and know ourselves as individuals within our own cultures and how we relate as members of or visitors to American culture, in particular. We all need to understand the worldview within which we must operate. To begin, I assigned the general introduction to SOL so that students could apprehend the central focus and critical methodology that would support their reading and writing in Units II, III, and IV of the course. At this point, I began really to "let my textbook support me." I made good use of the boxed questions imbedded in the text of the introduction for freewriting and journal writing. I also encouraged students to question the text itself and then attempt to answer their own questions either in group discussions or in individual journal entries. Since the introduction informs the reader of the constructed mythological underpinnings of all they know and believe, I consider it fitting that students question any possible mythological bases for the textbook authors' stance, as well. I want them to question everything!

Next, we read the introductions to Chapter One, "Consuming Passions: The Culture of American Consumption," and Chapter Two, "Brought to You B(u)y: The Signs of Advertising," along with selected essays from each of these chapters, to learn how "we" come to be products of our shared cultures. I found Laurence Shames's "The More Factor" (Chapter One) to be a real eye opener to the basic American myth and its all-pervasive influence on our national psyche. I then moved from the general principals of the myth to some of the manifestations. Finally, selections in Chapter Two, such as Roland Marchand's "The Parable of the Democracy of Goods" and Jack Solomon's "Masters of Desire: The Culture of American Advertising," helped all of us to understand some of the ways in which we disseminate and perpetuate that myth.

Working through these first two chapters prepared the students to write their second essay of the semester, an analysis for which I gave them a rather broad directive;

they could analyze a trend, a style, a fad, or an advertisement. Then, with Units I and II under our belts, we were ready to go on to my Units III and IV and *SOL,* "Part Two: Cultural Constructions."

My Unit III: Argument (The Position Paper)

About halfway through the semester we made the giant leap from subjective to objective writing, understanding that writing, either from "I" or "we," never allows us to be wholly objective. Moving to Part Two, "Cultural Constructions," focused our discussions and writing exercises outside of ourselves as we examined some of the issues featured in the textbook as well as some too new to have made it to the latest edition. Once we had worked through one issue chapter, reading the introduction and then at least three or four essays, the students acquired a basic understanding of how to address an issue. The textbook essays modeled for them how to examine an issue by presenting and interpreting data and then taking a position and supporting it. Chapter Six, "We've Come A Long Way, Maybe: Gender Codes in American Culture," and Chapter Seven, "Constructing Race: Readings in Multicultural Semiotics," generally are of interest to students because the readings deal with concerns that touch or have touched their lives. The readings in these chapters stimulated very active classroom discussion and some intense freewriting and journaling. Since students had by now liberated their writing from self, it seemed appropriate that their third essay assignment allow them a greater degree of latitude. Accordingly, for this assignment, they had the freedom to interact with any essay or essays from either one of the issue chapters we'd covered or to select an essay from one of the other issue chapters.

In addition, while we were working in this unit, students had the opportunity to begin integrating information from source texts into their writing (a skill that they would need to develop for their fourth major essay assignment). Furthermore, by interacting with one or more of the textbook essays, they learned not only to interact with other writers (by including a voice or voices other than their own in their writing) but also to work with the conventions of integrating and citing sources according to MLA guidelines. After that, it was onward to the final assignment of the semester.

My Unit IV: Research (The Academic Objective)

Now that my students had experienced taking a supported position using textual evidence in the argument essay, they were ready for the final challenge of the semester, the research paper. I never have been in favor of pointless research essays that are nothing more than information dumps; therefore, I required that the research essay make some kind of point and express a thesis, whether stated or implied. At this point, I made good use of SOL's model student essays located in "Writing about Popular Culture." The students had already read this section before writing their first essay, but I encouraged them to reread it each time they began to a new assignment.

For this assignment, even more than the previous one, I also relied on the textbook to supply the subject bases for the students' papers and to act as the primary research resource, as well. I did this with good reason.

Reason 1: To Plagiarism-Proof the Paper (well, almost)

Unfortunately, the plagiarism problem continues to exist, exacerbated by one of our best new research tools, the Internet. Not only do students turn in papers borrowed from friends or culled from sorority or fraternity files, but they also download papers from cyberfiles full of essays for sale. One way of circumventing the problem is to construct a research essay assignment that, like the argument paper, bounces off a textbook essay, thereby helping to ensure that students will not be able to submit a borrowed or purchased paper. I find that requiring my students to integrate two SOL essays in with their other sources to create the finished product allows little opportunity for plagiarism. This is another example of how allowing my textbook to support me helps me to maintain control in a critical area.

Reason 2: Creating Interesting Concept Connections and Facilitating Research

One thought-provoking way to construct the research assignment is to have the students not only address the issue itself but also examine the ways that media present it. Taking this approach, students can make use of both the textbook issue section they've chosen and one or more of the media-focused chapters back in Part One. With the textbook as their primary research resource, they have access to a number of essays from which to draw, and of course they can and must move outside of it to find additional material in the university's library and on the Internet. (I do limit the number of allowable Internet sources to two.) My students have turned out some extremely successful research papers using the textbook in this way.

I have continued to use *SOL* in subsequent semesters, always finding new ways to use its content and method. It's just like the mythical magic purse: each time I spend some of it, the expenditure increases rather than decreases its content for me.

Still More Support

Throughout the semester, the students can enhance their active, critical reading skills using the questions headed "Reading the Text" for reading journal entries. These questions encourage students not simply to read but to interact critically with the text to formulate their answers. I save the questions listed under the "Reading the Signs" heading for in-class work: freewriting, group discussions, group exercises, and other productive activities I otherwise would have to invent. These questions engage students in evaluating and analyzing the material content of the essay and their own points of view in relation to the material.

Here, again, I allow the textbook to support me. It is awfully hard work to come up with interesting writing prompts, whether for journal entries, freewrites, group activities, or formal essay assignments. Instructors spend many hours devising these kinds of questions, as did I during my first TA semester. It's a wonderful relief to let the textbook do more of that work so that I have the time, energy, and freedom to enjoy my job and to teach my students that writing need not be drudgery but an interesting, involving, and immensely enjoyable and rewarding pastime.

Finally, I want to reemphasize the point that accepting this kind of support does not amount to allowing the textbook to control my semester or me. I still make all the major decisions. I construct my semester, select the essays I want my students to read, make the assignments, and decide exactly how semiotic I want us to be. The choices are all mine. *SOL* allows me that degree of latitude. And what of the rhethorical art: invention, form, and style? In my experience so far, students learn more from reading good, interesting writing and then writing, writing, writing, themselves than they ever will learn from reading the dry passages found in many rhetorics and handbooks. What extra information I think they need concerning invention, form, and style I can supply from my own education and experience as a college reader and writer. We all can. We've made it this far: we must know something!

DEBORAH BANNER

UNDERGRADUATES IN GREY FLANNEL SUITS: ADVERTISING IN THE COMPOSITION CLASSROOM

On one unusually crisp Monday afternoon in November, a corporate behemoth took over my English composition classroom. Five creative teams vied for financial and administrative support as they presented advertising strategies for new consumer products to their supervisors. Each team unveiled a new product, discussed marketing plans, and debuted original print and video ads. Unlike most marketing meetings, however, this one ended in an awards ceremony, at which each group received certificates of achievement and rousing ovations. Also unlike most meetings, every participant submitted a five-page paper to the "Executive Vice President" — actually, me — at the end of the session.

It sounds elaborate, but to my students, that Monday was just another deadline for their fall class in composition, rhetoric, and language. They were used to odd pedagogical shenanigans — I had already impersonated a talk-show host, a fitness instructor, and an appellate judge — and my assumption of executive power over a fictitious conglomerate was, to them, the least quirky aspect of their assignment. For this project, I had required them to participate in the charade: each student took on a distinct role within his or her group, so that their presentations and papers were "reports" to the company's management from the "creative executive" or the "art director" of each campaign. Following the presentations, each student team submitted its ads along with individually written and revised papers; each student ultimately received a grade that combined the collaborative and the individual elements of the project. Without a doubt, this was a labor-intensive assignment for all of us. It was also one of the most successful class projects in which I've participated.

The assignment was inspired by Chapter Two, "Brought to You B(u)y: The Signs of Advertising" of *Signs of Life,* particularly several articles that I had taught before. Ads are great material for composition classes for many reasons, not least of which are their familiarity to students and the ways in which ads themselves can be examined for a visual "thesis" and "examples." I had assigned earlier classes Roland Marchand's "The Parable of the Democracy of Goods"; Jack Solomon's "Masters of Desire: The Culture of American Advertising"; and Diane Barthel's "A Gentleman and a Consumer" (all in Chapter Two). These three articles are excellent models for the mechanics of semiotic analysis, as well as for their presentation of arguments supported by reference to multiple specific examples. In particular, Solomon's article is helpful to students writing papers on advertising. Thomas Hine's "What's in a Package" (from Chapter One, "Consuming Passions: The Culture of American Consumption") is another article that supports this assignment well, and having students read Roy Rivenburg's "Snap! Crackle! Plot!" (from Chapter Nine, "American Icons: The Mythic Characters of Popular Culture") might be helpful as they design their own ads.

My earlier classes had discussed these essays in small groups and as a class; we had analyzed ads in small groups and as a class; and eventually, students wrote a paper on ad analysis. This approach was successful, but I had grown tired of my old plan. This time, once my students were familiar with the semiotic approach, I asked them to become ad executives. In groups of five, they were responsible for inventing a consumer product or service and designing a marketing strategy, complete with print and video ads. Along with the ads, each student was to write a five-page paper that referenced the articles in *Signs of Life* to examine his or her particular role in the group project. While I designed the individual job titles and separated the class into groups of five, students were responsible for assigning each role according to their own interests. This was more than a concession to my love of role-playing assignments; individual paper assignments were determined according to a student's position in the group. Each group had a Creative Executive, who coordinated the presentation and the advertisements with one other; organized students self-selected for this job within minutes of receiving the assignment. The Marketing Manager — usually a budding business major — was responsible for analyzing the target markets of the product and the target audiences of the ads. Public Relations Gurus examined the correspondence among the images of the company as a whole and those projected through the product and the ad campaign. Finally, the Art Director and Video Director took primary responsibility for analyzing the print ad and the video ad, respectively. Most students assumed their roles with great panache: one Marketing Manager promised in his paper that his team's product would "become the flagship brand for the corporation in the twenty-first century," while one Video Director requested my help in lobbying the campus media lab for permission to use their digital editing equipment, above and beyond the assignment's requirements. (The lab approved her request, and the resulting ad for a state-of-the-art health club was stunningly professional.)

I realize that the above constitutes a lot of work for two weeks. Then again, I work at an institution with remarkable technological resources for instructors and undergraduates. My students had free access to video cameras, viewing monitors, analog and digital editing booths, networked computers, color printers, and several different desktop publishing and photo editing applications, as well as university employees whose job it is to train and assist undergraduates in using these resources. With hindsight, however, a modified version of this assignment would work, with few adjustments, for students whose multimedia resources extend to a box of magic markers and a piece of paper. The assignment stipulated that no points would be added or subtracted for technological prowess or the lack thereof, and team grades were determined by the creativity and coherence of the ideas behind the advertising campaign rather than by any advanced graphics in the ads themselves. I received an assortment of print ads, including a construction paper and crayon collage, a computer-generated blend of text and scanned images, and one hand-lettered, hand-colored posterboard.

I had two goals for this project. Primarily, I hoped to help strengthen students' critical thinking, reading, and writing skills. By putting them in the role of producers, rather than consumers, of popular culture, I hoped that my students would take a more active critical stance toward their subject matter. By requiring a significant amount of teamwork, I multiplied the occasions on which students would examine, critique, or simply discuss their own writing and how to improve it. Beyond merely drilling students in criticism, however, I tried to engage those critical skills on a terrain where the class felt more at ease and more invested than they do with traditional academic analysis. Using *Signs of Life* gave me a head start here: students are already impressed and excited to be analyzing popular culture — a field that they often feel more authorized to critique than they do others. I deliberately structured the assignment as a "professional" project that employed several different media, in the hope that students might think of composition as more than a dull, academic rite of passage and see that clear writing skills have valuable applications in the rest of the world.

In previous composition classes, my students had examined popular culture as critical consumers but consumers nonetheless. Often, students felt so close to the objects under scrutiny that they had difficulty suspending personal judgments: for example, students who attend class bedecked in Calvin Klein logo attire rarely want to consider the semiotic subtexts of CK advertisements. They want reassurance that they look cool. Alternatively, out of a naive belief that "criticism" as such is inherently negative, some students resist imputing any motive to advertising other than genuine desire to communicate a product's virtues. By imagining themselves as advertisers, my students gained a crucial detachment from their material. Indeed, this is one of the reasons that the editors of *Signs of Life* suggest putting students in the role of advertisers for a day. Not only did my students take advantage of multiple possibilities for building signs into advertisements, but the depth of their subsequent analyses improved once they had recognized how far those signs and sign systems could extend. Because they were responsible for every editorial decision in creating the ads, students quickly dispensed with the obvious images — a smiling trio of women, for example — to focus on countless subtle signals working alongside the obvious. During one class period given over to team strategy, I overheard students arguing about the semiotic importance of the size and color of different typefaces, longer or shorter words in a slogan, the ethnic backgrounds of the people depicted in each ad, and the placement of each element in relation to the others.

Thus the smiling trio of women in one group's print advertisement was meant to signal feminist independence, appropriately enough for the product, which was marketed to women. Yet in the final analysis, the trio was also deliberately multicultural, dressed in casual clothes that bore insignias from prestigious universities, depicted in black and white, seated on comfortable couches, smiling at each other rather than at the camera, in a home and not outdoors or in a bar, surrounded by signs of professional success such as briefcases, cellular phones, and computers, and, finally, accompanied by a minimum of discreet advertising copy. Another group, selling sports sunglasses to the college market, designed their ad so that the sunglasses appeared in the center of the page, lit with a spotlight. Through the lighting, which they intended to connote museum exhibits or stage performance, they suggested the elitism, prestige, and attention-getting qualities of their product without including any text to that effect. Once students understood from experience that such signals are at least as important to a successful ad's composition as the depiction of the commodity itself, they ceased making the single most common undergraduate objection to pop culture analysis. In other words, they stopped saying, "It's just an ad. Aren't we reading too much into this?" and directed their energies at designing advertisements and writing their papers.

My students had fun designing their products and advertisements, and they zeroed in on some great marketing opportunities: one group dreamed up "the Air Executive," a comfortable shoe for businessmen, while another spotted an opening in the beverage market and created Belmont Beer for Women, named for Portia's hometown in *The Merchant of Venice*. Their general enthusiasm for the project carried over to their papers, which helped to motivate some extremely productive individual and peer writing conferences. While I have used several forms of peer review in previous courses, I sometimes fear that it can be a one-sided process. Peer editors have little invested in the outcome of their reviews, other than their desire that a conscientious reading will elicit an equally careful review from their partners. Yet my students tended to grow complacent with or tired of the peer review process over the term, giving cursory attention to the papers of their peers. With this assignment, though, each student's paper was linked to the group's final project. Every student thus had a vested interest in improving his or her teammates' papers, inasmuch as each member's understanding of the team's goals directly affected the group's success. Each student's paper was reviewed by two other teammates, doubling the amount of constructive criticism for each paper and ensuring that the group was in accord regarding the strategy behind the ad campaign.

Without exception, the quality of my students' writing shot up on these papers. Of course, not everyone received an A, but I was able to give the first A that term. Also, for the first time that term, every student received a passing grade on the paper. This was in part due to a significant amount of class time spent discussing the papers and the group project as a whole. During four different class meetings, at least thirty minutes were devoted to team meetings, so that students could plan projects and talk about papers, and we spent one entire class peer reviewing drafts. I discovered that students conceived of the project as a whole: during meetings that were technically scheduled for planning presentations, I overheard students brainstorming paper ideas; similarly, students used some of the time intended for essay review to work on video scripts or to discuss the layout of print ads. Because I required every team to meet me at least once during the planning stages, I could keep track of their progress and offer help wherever needed. Unexpectedly, these mandatory group meetings increased the number of individual student appointments: while reviewing their team project with me, many students signed up for additional one-on-one conferences to discuss their papers. Several students commented to me or on final evaluations that they had never before considered English classes to be that interesting. Such positive feedback was a real thrill on its own but also a gratifying indication that I was successful in achieving my less measurable goals for the project: generating interest in a field that students considered dull or irrelevant and applying student strengths in other fields to composition.

Most of my students were neither English nor humanities majors, and many felt alienated by writing and reading critical essays. Their levels of intimidation ranged from some students' vehement dislike of composition as a practice to the mental block that writing was a born gift and not a teachable skill that improves with practice. By requiring students to work with graphics and video as well as writing, I hoped to tap their creative sides and to uncover dormant talents for alternative forms of composition. One of the great strengths of *Signs of Life* is in its modeling of sophisticated written analysis with everyday objects and media, a feature that tends to make students feel more authorized to critique the material under consideration. I hoped to complement this strategy by combining writing, a skill with which my students did not feel comfortable, with related creative fields where they might feel more at home. Among other things, I discovered that my students excelled at creative multimedia composition, something I wouldn't have known had I assigned only written papers.

Discovering creativity in one area proved helpful in coaching students through other areas. Several students proved to be superb video directors, with a natural visual sense of narrative that they were not able to match in their writing. So we started discussing writing on their terms, comparing thesis statements to visual exposition, specific examples to shot composition, and revision to dubbing and editing. I stressed to students that writing, too, is a creative act, even when it is done for academic purposes. Composition skills are not only translatable across different media — from graphic design to written text, say — but are of equal importance in different media for the professional futures of many students. For example, a strong writer will design a web site better than someone who cannot support a general argument with specific examples. One student, whose level of academic motivation seemed exemplified by his confession (intended, no doubt, as a compliment) that mine was the only class in his schedule that he attended on a regular basis, turned out to be an absolute whiz at video and Web design. His paper, a semiotic analysis of the video ad by the sunglasses group, showcased a previously hidden ability to organize a convincing argument. Like many students, once he wrote about a subject of genuine interest, his writing improved. His argument was an analysis of the episodic nature of the group's ad, which was designed to mimic MTV videos, capitalizing on the short attention spans of the young target market as well as the aura of coolness and sex appeal that MTV projects. His discussion of and evidence for these claims were among the most entertaining, intelligent written work submitted that term.

Along with all of my lofty goals, though, I hoped that this project would help me do what every teacher wants: I wanted to have fun with my class. In this regard, the assignment was an unqualified success. Student presentations and ads were consistently entertaining and intelligent, regardless of the teams' technical prowess. Even the students who borrowed an existing commercial strategy were remarkably canny about the way they chose to do so. By reconfiguring a popular sales pitch to their own product, the student teams were able to reason out the mechanics of how and why particular pitches work. For example, one memorable ad campaign borrowed the "Got Milk?" ad format to sell a college-age dating service. The team was able both to defend the copycat style as a means of investing their service with an aura of wholesomeness, as well as to examine the applicability of the original ad series' signs to their own service, such as the implied urgency in the brief question, the tactic of coming right to the point, and the association of dating with an essential life function. Much more gratifying than the entertainment afforded by such presentations, however, was this project's unexpected effect of forging solidarity among my students, via productive, mutually supportive team relationships that lasted throughout the term. Of course, there was a dysfunctional moment or two — such as a group in which a student defaulted on his or her work or one in which an individual tried to impose his or her personal agenda on the rest of the team. Yet these kinds of glitches, inevitable with any classroom situation involving more than one student, were by far the exception. In each case, difficulty with one individual had the effect of bonding the other members of the team more solidly. With five members to each student team, this still left four people to execute a project, more than enough for successful group work.

I solicited student feedback at all stages of the assignment, reminding them that they were free to offer critiques and make suggestions for improvement, just as I would eventually critique their work. I'd use some of their suggestions if I taught this class again. For one thing, this project was more time-consuming than I had anticipated, for me and for the class. One student suggested simply allowing more than two weeks from start to finish, while another suggested that the video assignment could be modified into a skit forming part of the class presentation, thus saving the time otherwise spent filming and editing. Instead of submitting a video, student groups would turn in their scripts and stage directions. Students also observed that organizing meetings outside of class was difficult for anyone living far from campus. I had randomly assigned students to teams without considering the logistics of their meeting schedules; next time, I'd allow students to organize themselves by geography if that would enable meetings after hours. Finally, it's hard to grade individual students on a group project. Each student justifiably wanted a grade that reflected the work of the individual student, but it can be difficult to separate individual contributions to a group effort. Also justifiably, no student wanted anybody to take credit for work that others had done. My solution was to give each student an average of the group's grade for the project and the individual's grade for the paper. Of course, this had the effect of raising some students' final project grades and lowering others, but there was no case where a student who received a failing grade on the paper received a passing grade for the project. This was the result of luck, not careful planning: nobody failed the paper. Next time, I'd stipulate that a failing grade on the paper meant a failing grade for that individual on the assignment.

Overall, the advertising project was productive as well as entertaining. I learned along with my students and enjoyed the opportunity to work more closely with them than I usually do: I attended video training sessions with them and held many, many extra office hours to strategize ad campaigns with the different teams or to discuss papers with different students. My one caveat to instructors considering some form of this assignment would be to outdo yourself in offering positive reinforcement. At every stage of the project, I praised the work and the effort that my students were exerting, and our final presentations were followed by a small "Class Clio" ceremony, at which every group and every student received silly awards and certificates for achievements in "coolest name for a new product," "most likely to turn a huge profit," "ads so hip they're worth taping," and so on. Approximately half of my class were first-year students, and the rest were split fairly evenly among the upperclassmen, but all of them responded equally well to steady cheerleading.

Ultimately, the true test of a classroom project is the question of whether it is worth repeating. I don't need to think about that one. I'd do it again in a heartbeat — but I'd have to change at least one thing. Next time, I will dispense with the fiction of being Executive Vice President. Next time, I will be CEO.

PART ONE
Cultural Productions

Chapter One
CONSUMING PASSIONS
The Culture of American Consumption

We've made consuming behavior the subject of our first chapter because of the essential role that consumption plays in shaping American popular culture. The culture of consumption is linked most obviously to the topics covered in the first part of *Signs of Life* — that is, cultural products such as advertising, television, and film — but it affects as well issues such as gender and race that are raised in the book's second half. Thus, Chapter One serves as a useful starting point for a course, no matter which other chapters you include in your syllabus. You'll also find that consuming behavior is an ideal topic for beginning your course because it's a part of every student's life. This is true whether your students hail from wealthy suburbs and have lots of disposable income or are working single mothers struggling to make a life for themselves and their families. And it's true for traditional students and nontraditional students alike, those entering college straight from high school and those returning after a hiatus. The constant pressure to buy is an unavoidable part of their lives, even if not all are able or willing to respond to that pressure. If you like to start your course by concentrating on personal experience writing, begin with this chapter.

This chapter is also a fine place to start if you plan to adopt in an explicit fashion the semiotic approach that underlies this text. We've found that semiotics makes immediate sense to students when it's presented in the context of their own behavior. They know, for instance, that they are sending messages to others by their choice of clothing — and they're likely to admit it. Just ask them about the different messages they send when they dress for work, for school, or for a party. Or ask them how their friends would "read" them differently if they showed up driving a Miata or, conversely, a Hummer. The chapter's introduction emphasizes the link between consumer behavior and one's sense of personal identity to enable students to see that, in a sense, they've been semioticians all along.

The Discussing the Signs of Consumer Culture exercise, which asks the class to list and interpret their own clothing styles, is a great ice-breaker for the first few days of the term, when students may not know each other and may be a bit shy about talking in class. Note that the exercise forces students to distinguish between their own interpretations of their clothing and those of others. In addition, this distinction between personal and public meaning is important as students learn that academic writing is not simply an assertion of opinion but an expression of opinion through socially constituted conventions of discourse. In addition, this exercise can raise the distinction between a functional and a cultural meaning of an object. Students often are willing to challenge another student's claim that, for instance, she wears her ripped blue jeans "just because they're comfortable." Someone in the class inevitably will point out that jeans can be purchased ripped for fifty dollars, or that they project a cool image, and so on.

Students may be somewhat more resistant to the issue raised in the "Exploring the Signs of Consumer Culture" question, which asks them to reflect on the importance of consumer products in their lives. Because Americans still cling to the belief that one's identity is a highly individualized matter of soul and spirit, it's understandable that students may feel uncomfortable with the claim, made explicitly in the introduction and implicitly in many of the readings, that "you are what you consume." Ask students to volunteer to share their responses in class, and use them to trigger a discussion of the relative importance of consumer objects and other matters in their lives. You might want to return to this issue later in the term, especially after covering some of the chapters from the second half of the book, which show how even serious issues can be commodified in American culture. It would be particularly interesting to revisit the issue after discussing Chapter Seven, "Constructing Race: Readings in Multicultural Semiotics." Race is deeply connected to one's sense of personal identity and selfhood, and it is increasingly being appropriated to peddle everything from clothing to universities (check your college catalog for calculated images of multiculturalism).

The "Reading Consumer Culture on the Net" exercise should allow your students to have some fun in interpreting the mythology of American consumerism. You can ask your students to explore home-shopping networks and auction Web sites either individually or in small groups; they can visit the addresses suggested in the exercise, but by all means invite them to explore other sites as well. Students may not be instinctively analytical when visiting these sites because shopping is such a common behavior; you might prepare them by asking them to look at the products advertised (are they necessities? luxuries?), the images used to make those products seem desirable, and, particularly, the target market (typically women). If you ask your whole class to complete this exercise, try assigning small groups a different site and then ask your students to compare their findings in class. One final note: this exercise works perfectly with the Anne Norton selection.

The chapter covers a range of consumer objects and behaviors, and if pressed for time you could focus on the ones you feel your students could easily relate to. The selections by Laurence Shames and by John de Graaf, David Wann, and Thomas H. Naylor provide a general framework for analyzing consumerism — the former relates American frontier history to our desire for more goods and services, while the latter sees Americans as pathologically addicted to shopping. For two selections that focus more particularly on consumers' behavior, assign Anne Norton, who argues that shopping malls and catalogues operate as sign systems designed to stimulate consumption, and Rachel Bowlby, who analyzes the shopping experience as a binary set of images (nightmare versus liberation). A suite of four selections addresses different categories of consumer objects — objects that are all semiotically rich in significance. Thomas Hine studies a part of everyday life that's often overlooked in academic study — the semiotics of packages — while Fred Davis turns his attention to the packaging used to adorn our bodies, clothing; his focus on blue jeans should appeal to students of any demographic group. Joan Kron analyzes how home decor works as a sign of personal and group identity, and David Goewey examines the current taste for SUVs as an indicator of a cultural ethos. We conclude the chapter with a broader, more international perspective on American consumer culture: Damien Cave looks at the way marketers have turned terrorism, and Americans' renewed patriotism after September 11, into a source of profit; Benjamin R. Barber compares global capitalism and jihadic fanaticism; and Thomas L. Friedman reflects on the concerns often expressed on college campuses about globalization and the supposed Americanization of international culture. It's important for students to realize, we believe, that consumerism is not just about shopping and buying; it has serious implications for economic and political stability throughout the world, as the September 11 attacks so dramatically revealed.

LAURENCE SHAMES
THE MORE FACTOR (p. 56)

Shames attacks a cherished American myth — that the United States is a land of endless opportunity — so be prepared for some real opposition to his thesis. Because many students are attending college precisely so that they can expand their opportunities, they hardly want to hear that their hunger for more may not be nourished. Their response may also be complicated if they are recent immigrants whose lives have been directly shaped by this myth. In class, you may want to focus initially on the first part of Shames's essay, his discussion of the frontier myth of limitless opportunity. Your students are likely to be familiar with this myth from popular media; they could brainstorm examples of TV shows and films that perpetuate this myth. You might ask them to analyze as well the "Just What Do You Do All Day?" photo on page 70. Appearing first in a 1947 edition of *Life* magazine, the photo presents "the material record of one homemaker's weekly toil," thus making an interesting equivalence between domestic labor and consumption. Then move to the more troubling of Shames's assertions, his claim that America is "running out of more." This selection was published in 1989, so you could ask your class whether the current recession and drop in the stock market have altered the "hunger for more." If you have adults in your class, try sparking a debate between them and their younger counterparts, who may have had less experience in the working world. Politically conservative students might object that Shames questions the efficacy of a free-market economy, and they'd be right: it's just that Shames would see the free-market ideology as problematic. The essay could also be complicated by introducing issues of race and gender; the opportunities Shames describes have not always been equally available to everyone in our society.

The selection is particularly good for teaching critical reading and summarizing skills. The three Reading the Text questions ask students to identify some of the key concepts in Shames's essay; you could use these exercises to gauge quickly how well your students have grasped Shames's ideas. The first Reading the Signs question asks students to extend Shames's thesis into the twenty-first century; you might invite students to generate evidence both from personal experience and observation and from current political events. Because question 2 points to what is perhaps Shames's most controversial claim — that ethical standards have been destroyed by the hunger for more — it's ideal for staging an in-class debate. In preparing for a debate, students will need to anticipate counterarguments and develop specific evidence; be sure to allot sufficient class time for them to do this in groups. You may also want to combine a debate with a discussion of library research techniques (students could investigate, for instance, some of the recent scandals surrounding Enron and Arthur Andersen). Question 2, of course, could be adapted to an at-home essay as well. The remaining questions ask students to relate Shames's selection to other issues raised in the text. Question 3 is straightforward, asking students to apply Shames's argument to the Kron essay found in this chapter. Question 4 is more challenging and open-ended, for it asks students whether gangs share the hunger for more and thus can be considered typically American. You might ask students first to explore in their journal their assumptions about gang members; those assumptions are likely to shape their responses. Although often seen as countercultural groups, gangs also display a strong sense of territory and acquire consumer objects, particularly clothing, as badges of identity — characteristics that, in Shames's terms, can be seen as evidence of a desire for more.

ANNE NORTON
THE SIGNS OF SHOPPING (p. 63)

You can have a lot of fun with Norton's essay: it's a rich analysis of something most people take for granted — shopping malls and catalogues. The article begins in a somewhat dense academic style, but that style diminishes as the article progresses. Whatever your students' economic background, you can assume they're familiar with some sort of mall and occasionally peruse catalogues. Norton's selection works well early in a term, for it provides a wonderful opportunity for combining discussion of personal experience with an analytic interpretation of an accessible topic. Some students may resist Norton's claim that one's behavior can be so thoroughly manipulated by marketers, but ask them to consider specific examples that are close to their own experiences. Why do Victoria's Secret shops feature gilded and lacy touches? What's the image projected by that slick Gap storefront? Your students may balk at Norton's suggestion that malls appeal to women's desire for independence and escape from home; ask them to test her assertion empirically by performing a rough demographic survey at a local mall. What do their results suggest about the gender patterns in malls?

    The Reading the Text questions will enable you to see if students grasp Norton's central concepts or if they have difficulty with her occasionally academic style; they will also reveal if your students hesitate to accept her premise that an everyday activity such as shopping can be constrained by political ideologies and cultural mythologies. If they do resist this premise, ask them whether they respond differently when visiting, say, a Banana Republic outlet and a Target store — and why. In varying ways, the Reading the Signs questions ask students to apply or extend Norton's argument about shopping. Question 1 asks them to apply Norton's claims to window displays in a local mall; this question works especially well if they study the displays of at least two shops, preferably shops intended for the same market. Question 2 should trigger a great in-class discussion, with students comparing catalogues in small groups. (For variety, you might bring in some catalogues you receive; expect many students to bring in Victoria's Secret or Abercrombie and Fitch.) Question 5 is an at-home companion question that invites students to analyze closely one catalogue. For questions 2 and 5, encourage your students to focus on details. Why does the L. L. Bean catalogue include a golden retriever, not a rottweiler? Question 3 is ambitious, for it invites students to test Norton's gender-based argument by interviewing women of different ages. For this question, you might first want to discuss interviewing strategies — and the importance of interpreting an interviewee's comments. Questions 4 and 6 turn to the Internet, with 4 asking students to study the Home Shopping Network and 6 focusing their attention on a commercial Web site.

JOHN DE GRAAF, DAVID WANN, AND THOMAS H. NAYLOR
THE ADDICTIVE VIRUS (p. 71)

A brief and accessible selection, "The Addictive Virus" presents a slightly audacious but nonetheless compelling argument about Americans' "addiction" to shopping. Students can have fun with this piece. You might jump-start class discussion by asking students about their own behaviors as shoppers: Do they ever feel a "high" after a successful shopping trip? Do they develop "heightened sensations" while at a mall? Do they find themselves building what the authors call "personal fortresses" with their purchases? (Before discussing the article, consider assigning Reading the Signs question 2, which invites a journal entry in which students reflect on their own purchases.) To prompt honest responses, encourage students to think about product categories that mean something to them. Some students might initially balk at the notion of being addicted to shopping but then reconsider when they think about all the computer gadgets and upgrades that they constantly buy. Others may not care about technology but go ga-ga when visiting a store such as Aahs! that sells an endless array of trinkets, cute knick-knacks and stuffed toys, cards, and even some soft-porn doo-dads. For a lively class activity, try the exercise suggested in Reading the Signs question 3, which has the class brainstorm lists of products they have bought recently, then assess the lists for signs of addictive buying. We suggest this exercise so students can gain a collective sense of their shopping behavior and not be limited by their individual habits. You should discuss as well the authors' tone, which is sprightly, a bit tongue-in-cheek (to wit: "We're all crazy!"). How does the tone affect students' response to the article's argument?

After discussing shopping behavior, you can move to the authors' more debatable point, their analogy between "affluenza" and physical addictions. Expect students to accept shopping addiction with a small *a*; in other words, they may agree that it can be a compulsive, emotionally satisfying experience but disagree with the authors' analogy with conditions such as alcoholism and addictive gambling. This analogy is the focus of Reading the Signs question 4, which prompts students to evaluate the logical validity of this analogy. We suggest that students consult a medical encyclopedia for a definition of *addiction*; we're sure they understand that, although addiction is commonly seen as an abuse of a physical substance (alcohol, drugs), some behaviors can also be considered clinically as addictive (gambling). For a challenging essay assignment, try question 1, which asks students to compare Laurence Shames's concept of the "more factor" with the "never enough" principle described in "The Addictive Virus." Alternately, you could ask students to critique the two articles' presentations of fundamentally similar concepts. How do the authors' rather different styles, attempts at contextualizing the issues, and evidence affect the relative persuasiveness of their aruments?

RACHEL BOWLBY
THE HAUNTED SUPERSTORE (p. 76)

Bowlby's selection can serve as a useful companion to "The Addictive Virus," for while she acknowledges that shopping trips can be addictive, she complicates that depiction by analyzing shopping trips as sets of opposing experiences, nightmare versus liberation. But you may want to take some time working through this selection in class, because Bowlby's discussion tends to meander and the selection lacks an up-front statement of thesis. Indeed, you might sketch on the board a chart of the several sets of binary oppositions that, she claims, share a parallel logic. She starts by describing a visit to an IKEA that encapsulates her binary opposition: with the computers down, customers who formerly enjoyed the thrill of fulfilling material desires feel trapped and imprisoned. This binary opposition, Bowlby suggests, extends to images of shoppers that are perpetuated by marketers and that affect our behavior as consumers. Ask your students about these two images: the methodical, rational shopper and the more impulsive shopper who is susceptible to marketing ploys. To what extent are store designs geared for one or the other? In which category do students locate themselves? (To prepare students to answer this question, assign in advance of your class discussion Reading the Signs question 1.) Is the first kind of shopper really less vulnerable to marketing ploys, or is that perception, in itself, a form of flattery designed to encourage one to buy? Are they really distinct images? (Bowlby herself claims that an individual shopper can easily assume both identities depending on the circumstance.) You then should move to a parallel set of opposites, Bowlby's distinction between the department store (which she links to leisure, luxury, pleasure) and the supermarket (which is related to functionality, work, even entrapment). To make her discussion more concrete, you might look at magazines from several decades ago and examine the advertising: How are the two sorts of stores presented? What images are attached to them, and how do those images promote different patterns of consumption? We find her oppositions to be most interesting, and persuasive, in her concluding discussion of IKEA as a combination of the two forms of stores. Ask your students if they, too, have experienced both "leisure" and "work" in an IKEA. If no IKEA is located in your area, you can ask them about their experiences in a local shopping mall. To what extent is the mall set up to appeal both to pleasure and to function?

A basic analysis assignment, Reading the Signs question 2 asks students to assess Bowlby's view of shopping as a series of binary oppositions; you should encourage students to generate evidence drawn from specific stores that they have frequented. For assignments based on field observations, consider question 3, which has students visit and analyze a department store, or question 5, which asks them to visit an IKEA. If your class is emphasizing gender issues, you'll be interested in question 4, which asks students to assess Bowlby's contention that the image of the consumer is no longer exclusively female. For evidence, students could study media examples (magazine and television advertising would provide lots to analyze) and in-store and in-mall displays.

THOMAS HINE

What's in a Package (p. 84)

At first students may view packages as purely functional: we need them to hold toothpaste, or deodorant, or whatever. But Hine should open their eyes to the images packages create for their products. His selection is easy to read, and students are likely to be persuaded by his discussion both of the marketing decision-making behind package design (why are billions spent on packaging, anyway?) and of the cultural differences in packaging. Ask your students about trends in packaging design. Why, for instance, is Oral-B dental floss now sold in a translucent aqua package reminiscent of an iMac? Why does Pepsi seem to change its cans every few months? Whether or not your students accept Hine's notions, you can plan a great session by assigning Reading the Signs question 1, which asks students to bring a product to class. We've suggested that students all bring items from the same product category to allow for comparison of design choices. As an alternative, you might identify four or five categories and have small groups of students sign up for each. If you ask students to give brief presentations of their object, be sure to give them a strict time limit (probably just a few minutes), or else some students may not to have a chance to present. Questions 2 and 4 are similar in that they invite students to analyze the packaging of one retail outlet (with the latter question specifying an outlet with an explicit political theme). You can stage in-class activities similar to those called for in question 1 by asking your students to bring to class samples of the packaging from their store. Questions 3 and 5 relate the issue to students' own consuming behaviors. Number 3 calls for a journal entry on the appeal of packaging, while 5 asks students to interpret, through a stranger's eyes, the packages visible in their own home. Joan Kron's essay in this chapter is a natural complement to Hine's selection and can help students respond to this question.

FRED DAVIS
BLUE JEANS (p. 93)

You'll probably find that students accept the notion that clothing is a sign system: Just ask them about the different meanings clothing can have in the context of the office or school — or a date at a club. Were any styles banned from their high school, and if so, why? What did the forbidden styles mean to students and to parents and administrators? Fred Davis focuses on one of the most ubiquitous articles of clothing in American culture: blue jeans. Davis's selection is accessible, but be sure students don't overlook his central argument that jeans have occupied two contradictory sets of symbolic significance in American society: values that he terms "democratic" and "left" wing compared to values he dubs "dedemocratizing" and "right" wing. Note that this distinction is roughly parallel to that articulated in Jack Solomon's selection in Chapter Two, a nice companion piece to the Davis essay.

Students will enjoy Reading the Signs question 1, which asks them to bring a current fashion magazine to class, but be forewarned that they may have some difficulty applying the democratizing/dedemocratizing concepts. To help them, you might start with an issue of *Vogue*, which is likely to contain many examples of high fashion, and then move to the other magazines that your students bring to class. Question 2 calls for an update of Davis's essay through an analysis of current trends in the blue jean industry; students should take into account the current taste for ultra-faded, bizarrely cut jeans that seem to outdo each other in looking dirty. Question 3 is ideal if you are emphasizing the semiotic method, for it asks students to weigh the relative value of function and cultural significance in clothing choices. The last two questions invite students to study real people's fashion tastes, with 4 calling for a journal entry in which students reflect on their own preferences and 5 asking them to interpret the styles predominant on your campus (this last question could work nicely as a group project).

JOAN KRON
THE SEMIOTICS OF HOME DECOR (p. 101)

We consider Kron's essay one of the best in the chapter, both for its clear, lively writing and for its insightful exploration of how home decor works as a sign of one's identity. And students respond positively to her argument. Like most people, they probably have never considered the issues she raises but are quick to recognize the validity of her claims. Students may quarrel with Kron's implied criticism of materialism in our lives — especially if they stop reading after the Martin J. Davidson anecdote — but be sure they notice that she does not limit her discussion to American culture and that she is not entirely critical of people's use of objects and decor as a symbol system. Indeed, Kron believes that the use of material symbols and signs is intrinsically human. If your class includes students from a variety of ethnicities or nationalities, you might ask them to do a sort of cross-cultural survey of domestic decor and furnishings to see how different cultures make, in Kron's terms, "distinctions between ourselves and others."

This essay lends itself to questions and exercises that invite students to use personal experience; Reading the Signs questions 1, 2, and 4 all do this in various ways. Question 3 invites students to argue with or modify one of Kron's more extreme claims, that "To put no personal stamp on a home is almost pathological in our culture." The last question may be the most challenging. It directs students to Karen Karbo's "The Dining Room" in Chapter Five; the link between Kron's and Karbo's selections involves the way possessions can serve as signs of relationships, and you'll want to be sure your class discusses that topic.

DAVID GOEWEY

"CAREFUL, YOU MAY RUN OUT OF PLANET": SUVS AND THE EXPLOITATION OF THE AMERICAN MYTH (p. 112)

If you're emphasizing a semiotic approach, this selection is a sure bet for your syllabus, for Goewey provides a model semiotic reading of the most popular current trend in the automotive world. Not only does Goewey discuss the broad cultural significance of SUVs, but he clearly and effectively outlines the larger system in which they appear. A profitable class exercise would be to dissect Goewey's methodology — and to study the ways in which his inclusion of abundant specific details works to make his argument both vivid and logical. Even if you're not using semiotics explicitly, this selection is likely to trigger a lively response from students. Although some may balk at Goewey's historical analysis, few would claim that image and cultural association have nothing to do with one's automotive preferences. Ask your students: What sorts of vehicle would they like to be seen driving, and why? Why is it that some people identify totally with their cars? Note that, in its discussion of American frontier myth, this selection pairs well with the Laurence Shames selection in this chapter.

This selection is ideal for both personal and analytic assignments. A journal entry topic, Reading the Signs question 1 invites students to interpret the significance of their own car (or that of an acquaintance); this topic could be suitable for a personal essay as well. For straightforward analytic topics, consider question 2, which calls for a Goewey-style analysis of a different category of vehicles (sporty two-seaters, pick-up trucks, retro cars like the PT Cruiser, and luxury sedans all would be good choices because they have clearly recognizable cultural associations), or question 3, which sends students to automobile advertising for signs of the values and ideologies associated with particular car models. In working with students on such assignments, you'll want to make sure they see beyond the functional appeal of a particular vehicle (for example, an ad's performance claims) to the values the ad connotes. For an argumentative assignment, assign question 4, which suggests that students use interview evidence as support in a response to Goewey's thesis about the motivations behind SUV ownership.

DAMIEN CAVE
The Spam Spoils of War (p. 122)

You'll want to make sure students grasp the more significant points made in this very accessible article. Cave describes the flood of post–September 11 merchandise, from flags to terrorist hex dolls, and the ludicrousness of some of these products makes it easy to dismiss the phenomenon as just another cheap way to make a buck (see as well the political cartoon on p. 000). And although it's certainly fair to do that, you'll want your students to grasp Cave's more profound claim that the rush to produce and buy war-related merchandise is "quintessentially American." Ask your students to debate this point; for help in outlining the American consumerist psyche, suggest that they consult Laurence Shames's "The More Factor." In addition, they might interview people who, long after the attacks, continue to sport flag-related paraphernalia and ask them about their motivations and desires; see Reading the Signs question 3, an essay topic that could also serve as an in-class debate. Another debate topic is suggested by question 1, which addresses the proposal that patriotic scamming should be a crime. If you assign this topic, expect lots of discussion of the relative values of the right to free speech, the need for national security, and simple decency and good taste. To update Cave's references and argument, you could assign question 2, which sends students to the Internet to discover the current availability of post–9/11 products. Encourage your students not simply to report on their findings but to analyze them as well. What do their results say about the current national mood? What recent political and social events may explain any changes that they discover?

BENJAMIN R. BARBER
Jihad vs. McWorld (p. 126)

The global dimensions of American popular culture have become increasingly apparent in recent years, with works like George Ritzer's *The McDonaldization Thesis* (1998) exploring the profound influence of American-style consumer culture within and beyond our own borders. In the aftermath of the September 11, 2001, attacks, Benjamin R. Barber's pioneering analysis of some of the ramifications of this influence have assumed a special urgency, and your students should respond with great interest to his observations. Be sure that they understand that Barber critiques rather than endorses the common tendency to see international politics in the form of a simple us-versus-them dichotomy, a war between tribalism and technological modernity, for though he does introduce such a polarity into his discussion (especially through his provocative title), his point is to complicate, not propound, it. You might begin class discussion by asking students to describe in their own words what Barber dubs "jihad" and "McWorld"; this is an important first step because, although Barber's terms can refer to Islamist fundamentalism and to the McDonalds chain, they encompass much more than that. Indeed, the terms refer to a whole constellation of values, attitudes, and cultural practices, which, though typically seen as oppositional, are, according to Barber, interdependent and share an essentially antidemocratic core. This point is one you may need to spend some time reviewing with your students, because Barber's presentation of it is general and theoretical, not grounded in specifics. You can expect that most students would more easily grasp how jihad can be antidemocratic (they may know, for instance, that countries such as Iran and Saudi Arabia are run by repressive regimes, and the war in Afghanistan spurred a flood of new stories about that nation's tyranny), but some students may be puzzled by the claim that McWorld is antidemocratic as well. To illustrate how the marketing and advertising forces of modern capitalism can also have an antidemocratic effect, assign James B. Twitchell's "What We Are to Advertisers" (p. 205) as a companion piece.

Barber alludes briefly to some instances of corporate America's global reach, but some students may not be that familiar with this phenomenon. You might draw their attention to the photo of Muslim women using computers on p. 130 and to the photo of the Lahore, Pakistan, street scene on p. 135. In addition, students might do some Internet research on globalization; in June, 2002, for instance, the McDonalds Web site (**www.mcdonalds.com**) boasted outlets in 121 countries, with a link to each country that promotes how the host nation benefits from all those golden arches. Indeed, this Web site can be studied rhetorically, because it definitely shows signs of defensiveness about engaging in cultural domination (students should keep in mind that the Web site is a marketing device, and so corporate claims should be read critically). Should students want an alternative perspective, they can consult **www.mcspotlight.org,** which claims it's the most popular anti-McDonalds group in the world.

Barber's selection lends itself to thought-provoking assignments. Reading the Signs question 1 is straightforward but challenging: it asks students to view Barber's argument in the light of the September 11, 2001, attacks. Question 2 has students take on the question of whether globalization benefits the rest of the world (Web sites such as the two mentioned in the previous paragraph can provide students with specific evidence), and question 3 turns the issue around, asking students to consider the effect of other nations' popular culture on American culture. Perhaps the most heated issues are raised by question 4, which has the class stage a debate over the causes of jihadic hostility toward McWorld. To defuse possible tensions in class, we suggest that you assign students to groups arbitrarily, so it's clear that individuals are not necessarily arguing their heart and soul. For a textual analysis assignment, try question 5, which calls for a comparison and contrast between Barber's essay and Thomas L. Friedman's "Revolution Is U.S." (p. 132), an article that addresses similar issues but that has marked tonal and rhetorical differences than the Barber piece.

THOMAS L. FRIEDMAN
Revolution Is U.S. (p. 132)

With its focus on globalization, Friedman's selection makes a handy companion piece to Benjamin R. Barber's "Jihad vs. McWorld," but it's hardly a repeat. Friedman draws his own distinction between globalization, which once had a nationally complex dynamic, and Americanization, which is unidirectional. (You might look at the photo of the Lahore, Pakistan, street on p. 135 in this regard, for it illustrates simultaneously old globalization, in the Imperial Book Depot, and the new Americanization, in the Coca-Cola advertisement.) Because of various political changes, such as the end of the cold war, that distinction is rapidly fading, with Americanization supplanting globalization. Indeed, for Friedman, what's significant is not simply the influence of American corporations across the world but the inevitable exportation of American cultural values and ideologies that are carried by those corporations. That's why he opens with his "five gas stations theory of the world," an amusing analogy that rather wickedly caricatures the cultural values and social practices inherent in five different economic systems. You might start your discussion here, asking students first to outline, perhaps on the board, those economies and the values and practices common to each. (We enjoy Friedman's sardonic humor here, but some students may object that he is stereotyping cultural patterns. If they do, that's a good opportunity to address the relationship between stereotypes and generalizations and to discuss Friedman's rhetorical strategy in beginning with this rather flamboyant "theory." And such students might enjoy responding to Reading the Signs question 4, which invites them to assess the validity of Friedman's theory.) Then move to his larger concerns about how the tendency to adopt American practices essentially violates "social contracts" (para. 4) that are very different than our own. What are the consequences of this tendency? What does Friedman's anecdote about an Israeli youth's desire for a McDonalds' autograph from former U.S. Ambassador Martin Indyk say about the love-hate response to American culture?

Like the Barber selection, the Friedman essay is ripe for thought-provoking assignments. Reading the Signs question 1 has the class debate the extent to which America is responsible for globalization. We suggest that students interview international students about American corporate impact in their home countries; in addition, they might consult the Barber selection in this chapter and the Marnie Carroll piece in Chapter Three. Question 2 shifts the perspective and asks students to evaluate the benefits of globalization to America. Encourage them to consider both apparent advantages (more markets in which to peddle goods) and disadvantages (job loss for American workers). The last two questions allow students to take issue with or support Friedman, with number 3 focusing on a claim he makes about American values and 4 addressing his five gas stations theory of the world.

Chapter Two
BROUGHT TO YOU B(U)Y
The Signs of Advertising

Advertising has long been a favorite topic in composition classes, and with good reason. Students can write critically about visual texts that affect their everyday lives and that therefore may seem more accessible than written texts. In this chapter, we hope to enable students to go beyond the usual evaluative criticism of advertising to an assessment of how ads not only reflect but shape American society. We've chosen readings that do not simply interpret ads but that address the ways advertising uses the fundamental myths of American culture to shape a consumerist ideology. It's unlikely that students have encountered such a perspective in high school (where they may also have discussed advertising), so you can look forward to introducing them to a fresh angle on the subject. If you're emphasizing a semiotic approach, we strongly recommend including this chapter in your syllabus, for ads are a natural for semiotic analysis. If you're skirting the semiotics, you can still use these selections, for they can trigger careful, close readings of advertising texts no matter what the methodology. We've seen that students take to analyzing advertising quite readily, so you should encounter little or no resistance to this topic. Indeed, you and your class should have some fun with it!

Your students will need little preparation for discussing advertising, but because it's such a familiar part of their lives, they may need some guidance in talking critically and precisely about it. Providing such guidance is the aim of the Discussing the Signs of Advertising exercise, which asks that students each bring an ad to class and discuss their interpretations of it in small groups. You may want to review first the follow-up questions in the exercise, for they are intended to help students move beyond evaluative judgments to a critical analysis of how ads work. We suggest that, as students discuss their ads, you move from group to group, pushing them to be ever more precise and analytic. If you have time, ask each group to select one ad and present their interpretation to the whole class. The Exploring the Signs of Advertising exercise stimulates students' critical thinking in a different way: it asks them to create their own alternative ad and then assess their creation. Putting students in the advertisers' seat, we hope, will enable them to see how the complex rhetoric of advertising is constituted. It would work best if you suggest that students redesign an ad they don't like because of its ideology. We don't see it as a problem if students have trouble coming up with a new design, for they could then reflect on the tenacious power advertising images have on our imaginations and worldviews. We've made this a journal topic, but it certainly could be a more formal assignment. The Reading Advertising on the Net exercise asks students to visit *Advertising Age's* Web site for its compendium of Super Bowl ads. This question is meant to inspire consideration of how advertising has become a source of entertainment in its own right; after all, many a viewer turns on the Super Bowl to check out the ads, not the football game, and many ads, such as 2002's Britney Spears Pepsi ad, come with their own pre-broadcast media hype. If your students do not all have access to the Internet, try downloading the text and images for class discussion.

Here are a few tips on constructing assignments involving advertising. Be sure to require students to attach copies of print ads they may be interpreting to their essays; otherwise, you'll have trouble evaluating their work. Students can benefit if, early in the drafting stage, you review a few simple, precise terms. Words such as *copy* and *layout* would enable students to avoid such clunky phrasing as "the words that appear in the advertisement" or "the way the images are arranged in the ad."

This chapter approaches advertising from a wide range of perspectives. Several selections take a broad view, and we recommend that you include at least one of them in your syllabus. Roland Marchand is essential for a historical sense of how the mythologies exploited by American advertising have evolved, Jack Solomon argues that a fundamental American ideology is revealed in advertising's paradoxical adoption of elitist and populist appeals, and John E. Calfee offers an alternative voice that defends the advertising industry. We include inside looks at how the advertising business operates: Gloria Steinem exposes the surprisingly cozy relationship between advertising and journalism in the magazine industry, and James B. Twitchell reveals how marketers categorize and stereotype consumers. Two selections focus on particular consumer groups: Diane Barthel addresses male-oriented advertising, and Eric Schlosser studies the strategies used to get kids to want more goodies. The final reading, by Kalle Lasn, laments the ubiquity of advertising in our lives; closing the chapter, the Portfolio of Ads presents sample ads that you could use for class discussion or essay assignments. If you plan to use just a few selections, many of them pair up well with other chapters and themes. If your course focuses on gender, the Diane Barthel and the Gloria Steinem essays are essential readings. The Marchand, Solomon, and Schlosser pieces complement Chapter One, "Consuming Passions." If you're interested in critiquing the behind-the-scenes techniques used to stimulate consumer desire, Schlosser, Steinem, and Twitchell can be read in conjunction with Malcolm Gladwell in Chapter Five.

ROLAND MARCHAND
THE PARABLE OF THE DEMOCRACY OF GOODS (p. 150)

Students can't help but be experts in advertising, for they're surrounded by it in their daily lives, but they may know little about advertising's early history. The Marchand selection provides some of this history, but it's not just background: Marchand reveals the surprising continuity of ploys used from advertising's infancy to today. Although early advertising looks dated and old-fashioned — often amusingly so — the images it projects and the myths it exploits are still around. One way to make sure that your students understand what Marchand means by the "democracy of goods" and the "democracy of afflictions" (the point of the first two Reading the Text questions) is to compare the 1920s ads he discusses with their present-day descendents. Today ads peddling everything from Internet access to wine suggest that you, too, can live the good life, and ads promoting personal care products still invoke the democracy of afflictions (even the wealthiest eligible bachelor can have dandruff). To prepare your students for class discussion, ask them to bring some modern candidates to class (see Reading the Signs question 2); you'll want to be sure to discuss how the ads' use of these myths may have changed since the 1920s and what those changes reveal about American values and culture.

Reading the Signs question 5 asks students to apply Marchand's ideas to the Devoe paint ad on p. 157, while questions 2 and 3 ask them to do the same with ads they themselves have collected; they should have little difficulty with such assignments. You might preface such an assignment with an in-class discussion of the Pyrene fire extinguisher ad on p. 159; be sure students note who the "you" in the ad's title refers to. Questions 1 and 4 are more challenging because they ask students to grapple with more abstract concepts. To prepare students for them, you might first brainstorm in class (either in whole group or in small group discussion) possible responses and, particularly, possible specific evidence students can bring to bear on the topics.

JACK SOLOMON
Masters of Desire: The Culture of American Advertising (p. 160)

This selection is particularly useful for its examination of the mythologies underlying American advertising; if you're emphasizing semiotics, it's a must. Solomon identifies two basic appeals used in advertising — the populist and the elitist appeals — and illustrates them with abundant specific examples. You should find that students easily grasp the clear paradox that Solomon outlines; for that reason, this reading is ideal for analytic essays in which students apply this paradox to advertising that they have selected. If your students complain that some of the ads are dated (this essay was first published in 1988), challenge them to come up with their own examples (the task required by Reading the Signs question 1). We've noticed that these appeals are most commonly used in media that target a wide audience (not surprisingly, since such an audience is more likely to hold mainstream American values); a twist to this question would ask students to compare ads in general interest magazines and those intended for more specialized readerships. Reading the Signs question 2 shifts from print to electronic media, asking students to analyze the advertising that accompanies a popular TV show in terms of its vision of the American dream. If you're encouraging your students to take a historical view, assign question 3, which asks them to compare advertising appeals from earlier decades with those used today. As you explain this topic to your students, be sure to encourage them to go beyond describing the differences and similarities they see to analyzing the values and mythologies that underly the ads. A broader issue is addressed in question 4, which asks the class to brainstorm a list of status symbols and then study the nature of their appeals; this topic would make a successful essay assignment as well. Perhaps the most challenging question is number 5, which asks students to argue whether the populist/elitist paradox still affects American media. For this one, you might suggest that students work inductively — that is, they should study particular media examples first, then arrive at an argument — for what they discover may be surprising.

DIANE BARTHEL
A Gentleman and a Consumer (p. 171)

Gender too often is construed as a "women's issue," and to combat that misconception we include Barthel's essay. While occasionally addressing the gender roles that advertising imposes on women, Barthel concentrates on the images that ads encourage men to emulate. If your class is focusing on gender issues, Barthel's selection is a must. Expect her essay to stimulate a lively discussion: students probably will accept her readings of individual ads, but some may resist her larger argument about gender roles. Borrowing from Baudrillard (don't worry — she keeps the diction accessible), Barthel speaks of the "feminine" and "masculine" modes, concepts that warrant some class review. You'll want to make sure students understand that when she says "the feminine model is based on passivity," for instance, she's talking about social norms, not biological necessity (see the first Reading the Text question). Her striking conclusion, that men increasingly are allowed to adopt both modes in advertising and in life, is good debate fodder. In fact, we recommend that you encourage debate by, for instance, dividing your class into teams debating the validity of Barthel's conclusion and asking each team to collect evidence from magazines to support their position. As part of the debate, students could present their own interpretations of ads.

Students should both enjoy and be challenged by the Reading the Signs questions. Perhaps the most straightforward questions are number 1, which asks students to test Barthel's claims against a current men's magazine; number 2, which focuses more narrowly on Barthel's views of car advertising; and number 3, which asks them to analyze the gender roles in a magazine designed for either men or women. We've made the latter question a small-group exercise, where you can take advantage of gender dynamics by forming same-sex groups; if you have time, have each group report their conclusions to the whole class, and then interpret any gender-based patterns in the groups' reports. Question 4 sends students to Holly Devor's "Gender Role Behaviors and Attitudes" (Chapter Six) to extend or reflect on Barthel's argument; students should be able to detect direct links between the essays. Finally, question 5 is deliberately speculative, intended to suggest the power advertising has on our understanding of an issue as basic as gender. It would work well either before or after you've discussed the essay.

If you like to include audiovisual material in your course, a dated but still relevant film titled *Killing Us Softly* (1979) is an ideal companion to the Barthel essay. Addressing the ways women function as signs (of sexuality, passivity, even stupidity) in advertising, this film shows lots of sample ads and delivers a lively, accurate interpretation of them. It's never failed to trigger a strong response from our students, and you can compensate for its age by asking students to test its claims on current advertising. A sequel, *Killing Us Softly Again* (1987), is also available, though it's similar to the first; it's worth checking to see if your school's film library has either film.

ERIC SCHLOSSER
KID KUSTOMERS (p. 181)

Students often assume that they are impervious to advertising, because they cherish a self-perception of being logical, independent-minded consumers. And thus they sometimes dismiss as much ado about nothing critiques of advertising, such as the one by Kalle Lasn in this chapter, that skewer the industry. But Schlosser's exposé of the techniques marketers use to attract children may give them pause, especially his discussion of "pester power" and the use of focus groups as young as two or three that are intended to provide insight into children's tastes. Ask your students about the ethical implications of such strategies. What are the implications of encouraging kids to manipulate their parents so that Mom and Dad buy the latest toy or video game? What values are advertisers implicitly inspiring in children? Should two-year-olds be considered the same as adult participants in a focus group? An interesting class project could have small groups visit Web sites for children's clubs or product lines designed for children; students should study both the pitches and claims for the products and the extent to which the sites ask users for personal information (indeed, it would be revealing if students discover Web sites that violate the Children's Online Privacy Protection Act). Be sure to extend your discussion to some of the larger ramifications of hard-sell advertising to kids. What are advertisers teaching children about the value of material goods? Do students see any connection between such advertising practices and the "addiction to stuff" described in "The Addictive Virus" (Chapter One)? As you discuss these matters, keep in mind that, as Schlosser points out, children's advertising exploded during the 1980s — precisely the decade when eighteen- and nineteen-year-olds were themselves kids. Ask your students to recall their own experiences: Did they use "pester power"? Did their parents impose restrictions on their consuming behavior? What was their attitude toward consumption at the time, and how does it compare to their current attitudes and behavior as consumers?

It's a natural to ask students to analyze children's advertising based on this selection. Reading the Signs question 1 asks students to analyze the advertising that accompanies Saturday cartoon shows, encouraging them to see the relationship between the advertising and the shows (you'll find that often the two are indistinguishable). For a more focused analysis, number 2 limits students to interpreting a single ad. As is likely to emerge in class discussion, children's advertising, especially in its more manipulative forms, often triggers calls for more regulation to protect these youngest (and most vulnerable) of consumers. Question 3 has the class debate whether such regulation is warranted; we suggest that teams work energetically to amass examples from print and broadcast media and from the Internet and to use them as evidence for their position. Implicit in Schlosser's discussion is an approach to market research that parallels the techniques described by James B. Twitchell in "What We Are to Advertisers." Perhaps the most challenging question, number 4 asks students whether Twitchell's claim that marketing relies on mass stereotypes applies to children. We say this question may be challenging because we've seen that kid's advertising often appeals to a sense of individualism — "You're special!" — and students need to be skeptical when such claims go out to millions of kids.

GLORIA STEINEM
Sex, Lies, and Advertising (p. 186)

No, we didn't include this selection just for its great title! This is a long essay, but a must for any class that addresses either advertising or gender issues. Steinem exposes the compromises magazines — particularly women's magazines — must make when soliciting advertising. Forget about freedom of the press: the advertising industry makes tremendous demands related not only to its ads, as one might expect, but to editorial content as well. And Steinem documents these demands thoroughly. Some of our students have been shocked by this essay, claiming that their eyes have been opened to a practice they never realized existed. Some, insulted at being conned by advertising disguised as "journalism," have vowed that they'll now think twice about buying popular magazines. If you want your students to cover something fresh in your class, this essay is for you.

Note that this is an updated version of Steinem's now-classic essay. The major change is a preface, in which Steinem describes the many reactions to the original publication of "Sex, Lies, and Advertising," reactions that ranged from bitter sneering to outright celebration. You'll find this preface extremely useful for its creation of a historical context and for its documentation of actual readers' responses to a text. Be sure to notice that Steinem dubs as the "most rewarding response" the inclusion of her essay on college reading lists!

We've never had trouble generating lively discussion about the Steinem essay. Her writing is clear, concrete, and accessible, so your students should be able to handle the selection's length. A few students may be puzzled by the term "complementary copy," but you can ask their peers to help explain it. When assigning the essay, you might also ask students to look through magazines they have at home to see whether Steinem's argument about complementary copy applies to them (Reading the Signs questions 1,

2, and 3 encourage and structure such explorations). We urge you to ask your students to bring in one of their magazines and present their findings to the class. Be forewarned that some students have trouble distinguishing between copy and advertising. That difficulty actually proves Steinem's point, but it also means that you may need to spend some time covering the difference between the two. We've found that Steinem's claims hold for most magazines — certainly for all women's magazines, but for men's and special interest magazines as well (*Car and Driver, Shape, Cat Fancy* — the list is virtually endless). It holds true the least for general-interest magazines such as *Time* and *Newsweek*, but even there you'll see some complementary copy, and students could develop Steinem's discussion of why these magazines' content seems less influenced by the ad industry. Finally, question 4 asks students to explore the First Amendment implications of Steinem's revelations. We've made it a journal topic, but it could be adapted to a formal essay assignment as well.

JAMES B. TWITCHELL
WHAT WE ARE TO ADVERTISERS (p. 205)

Twitchell's selection should raise more than a few eyebrows, for he exposes the schemes that advertisers use to categorize the interests and needs of different market segments. You can initially have some fun with Twitchell, because many readers will instinctively be prompted to see where they would be slotted in the Values and Lifestyle System, a scheme marketers use to correlate consumer taste, personality profile, and financial resources so that they tailor their campaigns for their target groups. In which slots do most of your students (or their families, if they don't see themselves as having enough disposable income to find their profile) fit? Are there any patterns in the class's responses? Note that because students may have to reveal financial background, you'd do well to keep your survey informal and anonymous. (Reading the Signs question 1 has students write a journal entry in which they place themselves on the VALS chart and respond to their doing so.) But you'll want to move quickly from your testing of the VALS paradigm to the larger issues it raises. What are its limitations: Are there consumer groups that are not accounted for? VALS does not make explicit ethnicity or gender as criteria, but are ethnic and gender identities presumed? If so, what difference does that make? VALS essentially relies on stereotypes of consumer behavior. Do students see larger consequences in a multibillion-dollar industry relying heavily on narrowly drawn social stereotypes? And you should raise one counterquestion as well: As Twitchell himself acknowledges, such categorization of consumers seems to be an effective marketing tool. What does that suggest about the power of marketing campaigns not simply to get us to buy but also to adjust our behaviors, even values, to social norms?

Because Twitchell makes unambiguous claims here, students should have no problem responding to his essay. Reading the Signs question 2 allows students to address the question of whether the VALS paradigm accurately predicts consumer behavior; to generate evidence for this topic, they might conduct surveys of acquaintances' habits as consumers. Questions 3 and 4 solicit argumentative essays: number 3 invites students to analyze the values implicit in VALS itself, while the more philosophical number 4 sends them to the Eric Schlosser selection in this chapter and the Malcolm Gladwell essay in Chapter Five to argue whether the research techniques described in these selections are ethical.

JOHN E. CALFEE
How Advertising Informs to Our Benefit (p. 210)

Are you looking for a counterpoint to the generally critical view of advertising that appears elsewhere in this chapter? If so, Calfee's easy-to-read selection is for you. Treating advertising as a competitive tool in free-market capitalism, Calfee argues that ads help consumers by providing a "cascade of information" about not only products but also serious issues such as health and nutrition. Most students are likely to be skeptical of Calfee's attribution of essentially altruistic motives to advertisers. But expect some students, particularly those who resist academic criticism of the media, to embrace warmly Calfee's claims (indeed, some who resist interpreting ads may echo this essay in their claims that "advertising doesn't affect me; it just tells me about what products are out there"). If you hear this claim often, you may wish to return to our distinction between an object's *function* and its *cultural significance*. For an illuminating in-class activity, ask students to bring to class ads that they believe do inform to the consumer's benefit; break them into groups and have them evaluate the extent to which the ads offer only useful information, not alluring images or empty promises. You might have each group select the ad in their group that best matches Calfee's claims, and then discuss the group's results with the whole class (if groups have trouble selecting beneficial ads, make a point of discussing why that would be so).

    Although we don't buy Calfee's claims ourselves, his selection is useful for its alternative perspective on advertising; as such, it is ideal for pro-con arguments or in-class debates. Reading the Signs question 1 calls on students to debate on Calfee's central thesis, question 3 asks them to study current health- and diet-related ads to test his claim that ads serve the public interest, and question 2 broadens the issue to advertising in general. Given Calfee's emphasis on the health-related information that advertising supposedly provides, we couldn't resist asking question 4, which suggests that students research the history of cigarette advertising. Before the 1960s, the claims for the health benefits of cigarettes were explicit — a point raised in the few lawsuits against the tobacco industry that have been successful. If you wish to ground these issues in your students' own lives, assign question 5, which has students reflect on Calfee's claim that consumers "miss advertising when they cannot get it." If you prefer to make this an essay topic, you might assign Kalle Lasn's "Hype" in this chapter as well.

KALLE LASN
Hype (p. 217)

Do you have skeptics who proclaim that advertising doesn't really have much effect on them anyway? Or that people really don't notice advertising? If you do, you'll want to assign Lasn's strident condemnation of, in his words, "the most prevalent and toxic of the mental pollutants" (para. 1). Strong words, yes, but they are why we like his piece: he offers a brief, vigorous illustration of the ubiquity of advertising in our daily lives. Expect some students to scoff at the force of his language ("toxic," "no one will be spared," "the absurdity of it all"). But you should ask students why Lasn is so vehement, and why he uses the second person so often. And you should challenge them to address his examples of ridiculous ads and their larger implications. What does the proliferation of advertising suggest about cultural values? What does it suggest about the separation of public and private space (a question raised by the ads above the urinals Lasn describes in paragraph 5)?

The clarity of Lasn's position makes for a variety of straightforward essay assignments. Because Lasn describes the inappropriate placement of ads on a college campus, we thought a productive assignment (Reading the Signs question 1) would ask students to survey their own campus for the range of advertisements and to use their results in an argument about whether on-campus ads should be restricted. Because campus ads are so common, you might brainstorm in class categories of ads, both formal and informal, that they might find, being sure to not ignore unlikely places (restrooms, elevators, water fountains). As a warm-up or a stand-alone assignment, question 4 asks students to keep an observation log that records all the different marketing devices they see in a day (this question doesn't limit students to the campus environment). You can use their results to trigger discussion of the Lasn essay and as the basis for their own essays. If you want your students to gain a historical sense of advertising's impact, assign question 3, which asks them to compare Lasn's piece with Vance Packard's exposé *The Hidden Persuaders* (New York: Pocket, 1980) — a classic unveiling of the power advertising has on our daily lives.

PORTFOLIO OF ADVERTISEMENTS (color insert)

We felt that it was essential to include some ads that your entire class could share. You'll find that the ads are ideal for semiotic readings, as well as for discussion of audience, purpose, and style. And they relate to some of the broader themes, such as gender, that emerge throughout *Signs of Life*. You can use the portfolio in a number of ways. It's perfect for class discussion, because every student will have the ads in his or her text and can refer easily to details. You might break the class into small groups, and have each interpret an ad of their own choosing; as the first Reading the Signs question suggests, you might have the class vote on the ads they consider most and least effective, and then discuss the significance of the results. If students find any of the ads problematic or offensive, ask them what alternative appeals they'd suggest. How would they redesign the ads?

Chapter Three
VIDEO DREAMS
Television, Music, and Cultural Forms

Your students will be the experts when you cover this chapter. We've had students claim that their arrival at full "adult" consciousness dates from August 1, 1981 (the day MTV began broadcasting). We've had students proudly assert that they've watched every episode of *The Sopranos*. And we've had students narrate with exact precision the labyrinthine plot of the most confusing *X-Files* episodes. Although not all your students will be TV junkies, many will be (or were, in their early teen years), and they may be far more familiar with current music and TV programming than you are. Take advantage of their expertise by asking them to shape your class discussion. Your students are likely to know which current shows are the best ones to consider in light of Susan Douglas's essay about women's roles on television, for instance, or they'll be able to tell you whether today's female rappers follow the trends that Tricia Rose outlines. Your job will be to steer them toward writing careful critical analyses of the shows and videos they watch and the music that they enjoy. That may not always be easy. We've found that some students identify closely with their favorite TV programs or bands, and they can resist critical discussion of them because they may feel their own tastes are under attack. (The Exploring the Signs of Music Videos questions, accordingly, allow students to explore the impact that music videos have had on them.) Be sure your students understand that asking *why* this image or this story appears in a video or TV program is not the same as evaluating their worth as individuals. Indeed, you should expect the argument against analysis that claims, "But it's just entertainment." You might respond with the central semiotic insight that nothing is innocent. In fact, media products are designed precisely to appeal to a culture's dreams and desires — that's what makes them entertaining — and what you're doing is studying the nature and social significance of such appeals. You could study the images included in the chapter introduction — a scene from the first *Survivor* (p. 227), a shot of the Simpsons watching TV (p. 233), and a photo of Madonna in performance (p. 235) — and ask them how, in different ways, the three are constructed to appeal to their audience. Are any of them "*just* entertainment"? If any students think so, they are more likely to feel that way about *The Simpsons*; you may need to remind them that the cartoon's originator, Matt Groening, began it as a self-conscious skewering of mainstream American culture. And, for light-hearted prodding to view mass entertainment critically, discuss the Calvin and Hobbes frontispiece, which is dead-on in revealing the power of TV to create iconic status when otherwise none would exist.

The Discussing the Signs of Television question is further intended to nurture such a critical approach by asking students to go beyond a show's surface appeal to ask, "What is the program really saying?" The Reading Music on the Net question has a similar goal. By asking students to explore how their favorite artists are "packaged" on the Net, the question not only prompts them to engage in some semiotic interpretation but also encourages them to see the ubiquity of promotion and image creation in American culture. In addition, you could ask your students to visit MTV's site (**http://www.mtv.com**) and interpret what they find there.

To facilitate class discussion, you'll want to ensure that students all have seen the same videos or programs. Although more than 99 percent of American families own at least one TV set, some students might not be able to watch assigned programs, either because of work schedules or because some dorm residents don't have their own television. We highly recommend that, if your school can provide the necessary technology, you tape videos or TV programs and view them in class before analyzing them. That way, you can stop and study details or go back and watch significant scenes a second time. You'll find that useful because students won't always remember details, or the details they recall won't necessarily be the most significant ones. Don't worry about using all your class time. Videos are usually short (four or five minutes), you could focus on particular scenes in long shows, and single segments of TV programs usually provide plenty to analyze (a half-hour show typically translates into about twenty-two minutes, sans commercials). You should feel free to zap those commercials — unless, of course, you want to study the significance of what products are pitched to which audiences and how they relate to the programs they sponsor.

The chapter addresses both television and music, and if you need to cut the chapter, you might focus on one or the other. The first two selections, by Todd Davis and Steven D. Stark, offer cultural interpretations of two very popular shows (*The West Wing* and *The Oprah Winfrey Show*, respectively) and are ideal if you are emphasizing a semiotic approach. The next two selections, Susan Douglas's feminist reading of women's roles in three supposedly "enlightened" programs and Amanda Fazzone's attack on programs that supposedly "empower" women, form a gender-themed duet. Tricia Rose's analysis of female rappers could easily make this a gender-themed trio. Tad Friend's discussion of the tolerance for foul-mouthed language on TV raises serious questions about cultural values and tastes — and the conditions that make them change from decade to decade. Two selections address TV programming from a broader political perspective: Tom Shales reflects on TV's ability to respond to the September 11 attacks, and Marnie Carroll counters the common critique of American cultural imperialism by pointing out that, at least in Europe, American TV's influence isn't nearly as extensive as many American culture critics would have us believe. Rose's selection, with its focus on music, also works well with David Schiff's and Robert Hilburn's articles, which both raise questions about the common practice of ranking popular music, artists, and trends.

TODD DAVIS

THE WEST WING IN AMERICAN CULTURE (p. 238)

We lead the chapter with Davis's essay because it's a fine piece of cultural analysis. Davis's argument is that one of today's most popular TV shows is so popular precisely because, on one hand, it seems to address "important" issues but, on the other, it does so in nonthreatening ways. In a sense, Davis is arguing that *The West Wing* fits into a long American tradition of diluting the controversial and the pungent, of turning sharp Wensleydale cheddar into Velveeta. You'll find this a tidy, admirably clear essay: Stark raises his central question of why the show is so popular; he suggests various reasons, locating the show within both the system of "serious" TV programming and the real-life political context; he concludes with his own recommendations for improving the show. Most students should be familiar with this show, so before you assign this essay, you might ask them to freewrite on why it is so popular. Collect their freewrites; then, to stimulate discussion of the essay, ask the class to compare their freewrites with Davis's analysis: Are there points of overlap and deviation? How might students account for any differences in their responses? Then you can move to a discussion of Davis's argument, perhaps comparing *The West Wing*'s handling of political and social issues with that of other programs, such as *The Practice*. The selection also raises questions about the increasingly blurry relationship between media and reality, because the show stars a popular make-believe president at the same time that the real-life president used one of the most highly rated TV shows as part of his campaign (see the photo of George W. Bush on *The Oprah Winfrey Show*, p. 245).

VIDEO DREAMS

Because Davis's argument is clear and direct, it provides a good analytic framework for class activities and essay assignments. Reading the Signs question 1 may be the most provocative in having students consider the blurring of reality and fantasy: it asks the class to debate Josiah Bartlett's presidency and then to hold a mock election between Bartlett and the real-life George W. Bush. If students start talking about Bartlett as if he is real, be sure to discuss that after they've held their election. A straightforward question that triggers an argumentative essay, number 2 has students evaluate Davis's central argument, while number 3 broadens the issue by asking students to assess whether American popular culture in general has the impulse to champion the banal and the bland (Sandra Tsing Loh's selection in Chapter Four and Benjamin DeMott's in Chapter Seven offer complementary arguments and could be assigned to supplement Davis). If you'd like an assignment that asks students to generate their own investigation, try question 4, which has them poll *West Wing* viewers about their response to the show and then use the results as evidence for a critique of Davis's argument. For this topic, you might have students submit survey questions to you in draft form (you'll want to warn them about leading or overly ambiguous questions); you might also discuss with them the likelihood that viewers will initially have noncritical responses ("I just like the show") and strategies for generating more revealing responses (viewers might be asked to rank their preferences for individual characters, for instance, and then students could analyze the pattern of responses they see).

STEVEN D. STARK

THE OPRAH WINFREY SHOW AND THE TALK-SHOW FUROR (p. 243)

Expect this selection to test your students' ability to separate personal tastes from analytic judgment. Though some of your students are likely to have never thought twice about Oprah Winfrey, many may be avid fans — the sort who who eat the foods she says she likes or who read the books she recommends because, well, she recommends them. It will be important for both groups to see that, in this selection, Stark isn't making an aesthetic or even a personal judgment about the Oprah Winfrey empire. Rather, he situates her program in the context of the system of talk shows and teases out the differences in an attempt to explain why her program achieved a stature the others didn't quite manage. If your students are tempted to respond in only a personal way to the show (and not to Stark's argument), assign Reading the Signs question 1, a journal topic, to get that out of their systems.

This selection is ideal for argumentative topics, particularly those that address the value and appropriate content of television. Reading the Signs question 2 allows for a traditional pro-con argument on sensationalism in talk shows; for a more difficult topic, consider assigning question 3, which focuses on Stark's central assertion that talk shows have had a democratizing influence on television. A more narrow-gauge question, number 4 has students watch an episode of *The Oprah Winfrey Show* and write their own explanation of its appeal (you can prevent simple restatements of Stark's position by asking students to consider as well whether the show and its appeal have evolved since Stark published this essay). For a topic that engages current debate, try number 5, which asks students to respond to media critics who wish to "purify" TV. Be sure that students recognize an interesting political twist here: Whereas Stark cites conservative critic William Bennett as exemplary of this position, liberals have it on their agenda as well.

SUSAN DOUGLAS
SIGNS OF INTELLIGENT LIFE ON TV (p. 250)

We include this selection not just because Douglas's title echoes our own! We like Douglas because she offers an insightful interpretation of some of today's most popular TV programs — and she explores the mythologies that underlie them as well. If you're emphasizing gender issues in your class, be sure to include Douglas in your syllabus; this selection pairs particularly well with Amanda Fazzone's "Boob Tube" in this chapter and Sandra Tsing Loh's "The Return of Doris Day" in Chapter Four. Your students should have little trouble with Douglas's clear, accessible style, but expect a few students to complain that she's making a mountain out of a very little molehill. If some students do so complain, discuss with your class the personal spin Douglas adds to her essay: She's critiquing programs she *likes*, not those she hates. (Such students may appreciate answering Reading the Signs question 3, which invites them to explore their response to their favorite TV show.) To ensure a specific discussion of the programs, try supplementing the class's reading of her essay by taping a segment of one of the programs that she discusses; to save class time, you could watch only the parts in which male and female characters interact or display what Douglas considers stereotypical behavior. Such viewing would prepare students for the first Reading the Signs question, which asks them to support or oppose Douglas's thesis using evidence from the shows she discusses. You'll find that her thesis can easily be applied to other shows and even other media — her essay allows for great flexibility in assignment creation. Reading the Signs question 2 invites students to extend Douglas's concerns to other shows that portray women as professionals (*Sex and the City* is a natural for this question, but others would work as well), and question 5 asks them extend it to young adult shows. Films also invite an analysis à la Douglas; question 4 thus sends students to Sandra Tsing Loh's essay. Question 6 moves to advertising, where students are likely to find lots of instances of covert (and overt) antifeminism.

AMANDA FAZZONE
BOOB TUBE (p. 255)

Expect some students to be unhappy with Fazzone's selection, because she takes issue with some TV programs that, despite low ratings, have been favorites among young audiences, particularly female viewers. *Felicity*, for instance, drew much of its fandom from college-age women, and *Buffy the Vampire Slayer* became something of a cult classic among the twentysomething set. To gauge the lay of the land, you might begin discussion of this piece by polling your students about their familiarity with the shows she discusses and their responses to them. If you have some die-hard fans, you could remind them that cultural analysis isn't the same as personal appreciation. Indeed, as you discuss Fazzone's argument, you might ask what her real object of attack is here: Is it primarily the depiction of women on these programs, or is it assumption by groups like NOW that such characters represent empowered women? Expect some students to focus on only part of the evidence (for example, "What's wrong with Buffy's being pretty and sexy? She's in charge!"). Here you might discuss the traditional positioning of female characters as sex objects and encourage the class to tease out any differences between those portrayals and the ones Fazzone describes (to our mind, the differences are largely superficial). As a companion piece, Andre Meyer's "The New Sexual Stone Age" in Chapter Six provides additional evidence, drawn from other media, of female stars whose ostensibly empowered surfaces cover an essentially retrograde core. In addition, Fazzone's selection pairs well with Susan Douglas's essay, with Douglas decrying the undercutting of the professional roles sometimes accorded women characters on prime-time TV and Fazzone lambasting ostensibly strong female characters who have been championed as feminist role models. To discuss both essays, you might have the class first brainstorm on the board shows that feature prominent female lead characters; then ask the class to categorize the characters who exemplify Fazzone's or Douglas's arguments, as well as those who don't illustrate either position. Then ask the class to analyze their results: What do they say about trends in the depiction of women on TV? Have there been changes since these articles were written?

Fazzone's essay allows for focused, straightforward analysis and argumentative topics. Reading the Signs question 1 asks students to apply Fazzone's argument to the very popular *Sex and the City* (you might refer students to the discussion of that program in the introduction to Chapter Six, "We've Come a Long Way, Maybe: Gender Codes in American Culture"), while number 3 invites them to select one of the shows Fazzone discusses and to analyze it. For a mind-stretching exercise, number 2 asks small groups of students to devise a show that Fazzone would approve of; we suggest that groups present their concept to the class, being sure to make explicit exactly what criteria they believe Fazzone would support (she doesn't directly say in the article, and identifying these criteria accurately would make for a test in close reading and interpretation). A broader question, number 4 has the class debate the postfeminist tendency to emphasize female sexuality; this could be an essay assignment as well. In either case, students might research both traditional feminist and postfeminist writers to learn their positions on this issue.

TAD FRIEND

You Can't Say That (p. 258)

It's been more than thirty years since George Carlin made audiences howl with laughter with his classic routine "The Seven Words You Can't Say on Radio," but while ordinary American language today is freer — or more expletive-filled — than ever before, network television is still rather nervous about the matter. Your class is bound to be amused by Tad Friend's slightly arch, but definitely serious, report on the way the networks police the language on their shows in the age of *The Sopranos* and other cable programs in which the dialogue goes where NBC, ABC, and CBS fear to tread. Friend's article reveals a far more profound point, however, than the more superficial matter of whether someone is going to say "bullshit" on TV; the real issue here, as Michel Foucault would have put it, is the power to restrict discourse in general. Most Americans, and especially your students, believe that they have absolute freedom of speech, but point out, even as they discuss Friend's piece, just how reluctant they may be to use certain words in class that they may use all the time at home or with their friends. (We've had students write "s*?@#" when quoting from an assigned reading that didn't hesitate to write out the word.) Someone may even say something like "pardon my French" before or after using a common expletive; if so, have the class analyze why they may feel it necessary to apologize for using certain words.

It might be helpful to instruct your class about the historical nature of restricted speech. In the Middle Ages, the blasphemous invocation of the Lord's name by Christians was particularly forbidden; this led to such curse-dodging neologisms as "zounds" (short for "by God's wounds") and "bloody" (short for "by my Lady), which are still popular today. References to body parts and farting were not so taboo then (think of Chaucer's "The Miller's Tale") and became taboo only in the Reformation era. "Damn" and "hell," once taboo words (they still were in our childhoods, at least), are now quite acceptable, while other once acceptable words, especially those that refer to groups of people, are not. Though you may not want anyone in your class to actually utter such words aloud (they really are quite forbidden), you may want to raise the point to demonstrate that discourse is always being policed, but we tend to be most aware of the fact with words that are on the verge of breaking out of confinement — like the ones Tony Soprano uses with abandon.

Reading the Signs question 1 gives your students a chance to write an op-ed spiece expressing their opinions about linguistic censorship when it comes to television programming. Question 2 looks at the broader issue of content, inviting your class to debate whether television should be obliged to represent ethnic minorities in certain socially approved ways. Number 3 calls for a critical essay analyzing the nature of the television standards departments on which Friend reports, asking your students to decode whether such operations are cultural archaisms or preservers of important cultural values. And question 4 asks your students to think about the broader field of American values that television's contortions over acceptable diction illuminate.

TRICIA ROSE
Bad Sistas (p. 266)

Your students are likely to be quite familiar with the controversies surrounding male rappers, and many may have full defenses ready for their favorite rap stars. But often overlooked in the debates about rap are the female rappers — which is precisely why we've included this selection. You'll find Tricia Rose's "Bad Sistas" useful for a number of reasons. Her analysis of several female raps is implicitly semiotic, and you could use her essay as a model of how to defend an argument by citing specific details from an imagistic and musical text. She also asserts a clear, though controversial, argument, and that alone can trigger lots of debate about the gender roles represented in both female and male rap songs (Reading the Signs question 1 prompts a comparison of the two). As you discuss gender roles, you should turn your students' attention to the photo of Salt 'N' Pepa on p. 275. How do clothing, expression, and body language combine to create an image for the group? Be aware that some sensitive issues may be raised in class discussion: Rose sees female rap artists as challenging the depictions of women perpetuated in male raps, and this position points to both gender and ethnic tensions. If discussion gets heated, try to defuse things by narrowing the discussion, perhaps to one of the raps Rose describes. You might also ask students to share with the class their responses to Reading the Signs question 2, which invites students to write a "screenplay" for a video that depicts their gender in a way that they like. We've made this question a journal topic, but it's workable as an essay or even as a group assignment.

Rose's essay lends itself to straightforward analysis topics as well. Question 3 asks students to analyze a video of their own choice using Rose's argument. A more philosophical question, number 4 asks the class to discuss why popular culture tends to disguise traditional gender roles with a superficial feminist slant. Your students' comments will necessarily be speculative, but a discussion of the appeal of particular pop culture examples may move them closer to a real understanding of American values and attitudes toward gender.

DAVID SCHIFF
The Tradition of the Oldie (p. 276)

If you're considering skipping this essay because you don't feel your students know or care about the oldies, think again, for Schiff raises broader, meaty questions about both elite and popular taste and ways *popular* came to be defined. In his analysis of National Public Radio's top 100 musical compositions of the twentieth century, he finds, to some surprise, that it is the oldie, that rules the list. Before you assign this selection, you might poll the class for their own choices, then compare your results with NPR's (they will likely be quite different). Ask your students about the legitimacy of NPR's ballotting process, which Schiff describes in some detail. To what extent did the process itself lead the results in one direction? You might also ask about the legitimacy of any top 100 list, which tends to be based on not random samples but on self-selected participants who have an avid fan's stake in the outcome. You might point out to students that these lists are, in part, a marketing tool for their creators: radio stations know, for example, that they will gain a larger listenership when they broadcast the top ten (or whatever), and they also know that the process of voting increases listeners' identification with a certain station — they become personally invested in what is broadcast. Do your students participate in creating such lists, whether on the Internet, in magazines, or on the radio? What is their motivation? What effect does the list have on their consumption of popular music: Does it broaden the range or does it conversely tend to narrow it (because radio stations so often play music that will be a "sure bet" with their particular listenership)? What difference, especially in the era of MP3, does such list creation make?

As Schiff notes, it's likely that college students would have a different response to the NPR list than he does, since they may be unfamiliar with many of the oldies on the list and are likely to be less sensitive to the relative absence of classical compositions. To prepare for discussion, you might download some of the oldies that won and play them in class. Ask your students whether they illustrate the appeal to nostalgia and emotionalism that Schiff claims characterizes them — and, if so, why such an appeal would be so influential. Such an exercise could be good preparation for Reading the Signs question 2, which has students examine the NPR 100 (available online) and to analyze the cultural values implicit in the results. (Alternatively, you might put a selection of songs on reserve in your school's music library.) Schiff's article lends itself to being revised by a different generation; students are likely to enjoy question 1, which has small groups brainstorm their lists of top post-war musical compositions (note that we specify this time period but fully expect many students to start with the 1990s). Have the groups compare their lists, both with NPR's and with classmates'. How can they account for changes in musical taste? In differences within the class? Question 3 asks students to address whether such lists are valid; to develop their responses, they might study not only NPR's methodology but that of magazines or other radio stations. Finally, question 4 has students to consider whether commercial forces are responsible for displacing classical music from America's airwaves. To prevent a simplistic response (for example, "Classical music isn't played because people don't like it"), we suggest that students spend some time listening to a classical station, visiting its Web site, and interviewing classical music fans (you may have some in your class). Students may be surprised to see the passion that devotees have for this form of music.

ROBERT HILBURN
THE NOT-SO-BIG HIT SINGLE (p. 281)

Hilburn's selection pairs well with David Schiff's "The Tradition of the Oldie," for both authors consider how it is that the popular becomes popular. Schiff take the long view in discussing NPR's top 100 of the twentieth century; Hilburn takes a shorter view, considering how it is that this week's No. 1 single gains that status. He argues that changes in the record industry — singles are no longer snapped up by listeners as they were in the 1960s, for instance — and the movement to ultrasegmentation of the radio audience have rendered the No. 1 status virtually meaningless. To make sure your students understand why this is so, ask them to name all the formats of music that they know, then have them compare their list with that from the 1960s (they could visit the school library's microfiche archive and look for the Saturday or Sunday entertainment section of a local or national newspaper, which is where the top ten singles were listed as news). In this era of crossover artists — an appelation given to musicians who appear in anything but their "home" formats — they may be surprised that Gladys Knight could share the same space as Tom Jones and the Who. You might also discuss why we consider No. 1 to be important anyway — and the extent to which such ratings serve a marketing purpose for the record industry.

Hilburn's selection is ripe for assignments that go beyond the immediate range that he establishes. Reading the Signs question 1 asks students to research a parallel phenomenon, the history of TV broadcasting, that is marked by a similar trend toward niche marketing. Be sure your students consider the impact of cable in responding to this question. Question 2 shifts students' attention to the effect of No. 1 status, asking them to poll music fans about the role the ratings game has in their consumption of music. Question 3 has students assess a change in the music industry that Hilburn neglects — the advent of downloadable music from the Internet — while number 4 invites students to consider whether noncommercial radio stations, such as your university's station, have greater freedom in programming than do commercial stations.

One warning: students might bristle at Hilburn's opening salvo, directed at Mariah Carey, but ask them what his point is. He's not simply attacking her ability (in fact, he does lob some praise her way), but he is using her as an illustration of the changing patterns in the music industry that he is assailing.

TOM SHALES
RESISTING THE FALSE SECURITY OF TV (p. 285)

Tom Shales's tone in this brief selection is sarcastic, even flip at times, but don't let that get in the way of addressing the more serious questions that he is raising. Essentially Shales is speculating on the range of functions television can serve in modern American culture. Entertainment, of course. But while Shales doesn't articulate alternate functions precisely, he implicitly would like to see TV serve as a social and political conscience as well, as a medium that can keep public attention directed to the "uncomfortable" as it allows for the profusion of the banal and the trivial. Ask your students: Is this is a laudable purpose of television? More problematically, is it possible for this to happen? If so, what changes in media business practices — and in audience taste and values — would have to occur?

Shales's piece is useful for assignments that address the place of television in American culture. Reading the Signs question 1 allows for a personal response to Shales's focus on TV's coverage of the September 11 attacks, while number 2 asks them to respond more analytically, this time assessing Shales's prediction that TV programming may get a bit more serious after the attacks. To demonstrate their arguments, students should base their essays on a careful consideration of current programming trends. Question 3 sends students to Damien Cave's selection in Chapter One to address the commercial exploitation of the 9/11 attacks (TV participated in it along with the Internet sources Cave describes). Perhaps the most challenging question, number 4 has students reflect on the power of visual images, especially in light of the events of 9/11. To develop their ideas, students might revisit the September 11 portfolio starting on p. 19. Many of those images will be familiar to students; how does their response to them now compare to seeing such images in the fall of 2001?

MARNIE CARROLL
American Television in Europe (p. 288)

It's a bit of a cliché that America's strongest export is its popular culture: McDonalds and Coca-Cola, blue jeans and Madonna. And there's a tendency among culture critics to see that ability to export popular culture as omnipotent: the world is being taken over by MTV, the argument goes, and other cultures and ways of life are being annihilated in the process. Although there's certainly some truth to that charge, it can be overstated, as Marnie Carroll points out in this interesting article from the online journal *Bad Subjects*. Carroll does not deny that American popular culture has been highly influential abroad; it's just that such influence does not necessitate erasure of native culture. Be sure your students note one of the strengths of her selection: the abundance of specific, telling details that demonstrate that European culture is surviving despite the onslaught of *Friends* and *Frasier*. To contextualize Carroll's discussion, you might assign her selection along with Benjamin R. Barber's "Jihad vs. McWorld" and Thomas L. Friedman's "Revolution Is U.S.," both in Chapter One. As your students discuss the influence of popular culture on their own lives, encourage them to extend the discussion to its effect on other nations. What are the drawbacks and advantages of cross-cultural exchange? Is it really as unidirectional as some critics fear? What are the larger political ramifications (Barber in particular can provide context for this question). Reading the Signs question 4 calls for an argumentative essay about these questions and has students refer to both Barber and Friedman.

You'll find that Carroll's selection yields lots of provocative assignments that can focus on a range of cultural issues. Reading the Signs question 1 asks students to evaluate the validity of Carroll's argument by having them analyze the TV programming schedule of another country (they can find one on the Internet), while question 5 asks them to perform the same task, this time by studying popular magazines from other countries (a selection should be available in your school's library). Another research question, number 3, asks them to argue whether rock 'n' roll is an example of the American cultural hegemony that critics so often decry (be sure students don't forget about the British invasion of the 1960s as they respond to this question). We've framed number 2, about why so much TV programming imported from Britain is "high cultural," as a discussion topic, but that could make a good essay topic as well.

Chapter Four
THE HOLLYWOOD SIGN
The Culture of American Film

It's not surprising that writing instructors have long used films as texts for student analysis, for the best films can offer the complexity, narrative structures, characters, and symbol systems of a novel or story. Film has also been a favorite subject of semiotic analysis, and with good reason. Movies are rich sign systems, deliberately designed to appeal to an audience's values and desires, both reflecting and shaping a society's dreams. We find that using a semiotic approach can help students make the leap from writing simply their judgments of movies — why they like a particular film — to writing critical analyses of them. Because movies are so much a part of their lives, it's sometimes difficult for students to interpret them critically. By providing an analytic framework, this chapter is designed to help them do just that. The Exploring the Signs of Film question asks students to examine their favorite films, reflecting on what their personal preferences reveal about their own tastes, values, and beliefs. In essence, students will explore how their cinematic tastes serve as signs of their individual identity. The Discussing the Signs of Film question looks at film as a broader social phenomenon, this time asking them to consider why blockbuster hits achieve such a status. For this question, have your class identify the most recent megahits, locate the films in the context of other popular fads, and consider the social values and ideologies that the films manipulate. It's worth asking students to consider how Hollywood's image-making machine works its magic on its own products; accordingly, the Reading Film on the Net exercise invites students to study the Web site of a recent film or the posters that advertise films. Students should consider this question: How does the packaging of a film affect a viewer's understanding of its meaning?

As with Chapter Three on television and music, it's useful to structure class discussion around a common text but given time constraints, you might find it trickier to watch an entire feature film in class. Some movies are ninety minutes long, so if your class runs in a two-hour block you probably can watch one movie in class. If that's not an option, consider assigning a current film for homework, or check to see if your campus has a film series that would enable the class to see the same film (usually at a discounted rate). Your students are likely to possess a tremendously high level of cinematic literacy — so high that it may pose a problem. When discussing a movie, you may find it necessary to steer students away from celebrity worship. Among themselves, they're used to talking about what film a particular actress has appeared in recently or what a certain actor earned for a film; at times, we've just had to say that celebrity gossip isn't the same as a critical discussion. You may also have to remind students that a public relations spin on a movie isn't the same as an objective analysis of it. The fact that Madonna says she is "telling all" in *Truth or Dare* (1991), for example, doesn't mean that it's the case. You'll be able to keep students on track if you remind them of that semiotic question "Why?" Keep at them to ask why this plot twist, or why a male rather than a female character, or why a black actor for this role: you'll have them on their way to writing sharp analytic papers.

Because the readings in the chapter address various myths that influence films, you'll find the chapter easy to adapt to your course's focus and students' interests. Robert B. Ray provides a broad framework for examining Hollywood archetypes, so we strongly recommend that you include his essay in your syllabus. Alternately, Linda Seger's selection outlines the "universal" story lines that give shape to the mythologies underlying many popular films. If you need to cut the chapter, you can do so according to the themes you're emphasizing. Gary Johnson focuses on the iconography of the

Western, the Sandra Tsing Loh and Jessica Hagedorn selections focus on gender issues, and the Michael Parenti selection examines social class. Susan Bordo and Vivian C. Sobchack provide cultural analysis (their selections are valuable for a semiotically centered course); the Hagedorn and Todd Boyd selections are perfect for a class addressing multicultural issues. Patrick Goldstein concludes the chapter with a reflection on whether it's time Hollywood got serious after the devastation of September 11.

ROBERT B. RAY
THE THEMATIC PARADIGM (p. 308)

Ray's selection has been one of the most frequently assigned in the earlier editions of this text — and that's no surprise. It's useful no matter what films your class analyzes, and whether or not you emphasize semiotics, because it focuses on an essential pattern of protagonists in American films: the outlaw and the official heroes. This pattern is by no means limited to Westerns. These protagonists are found in action-adventure, mystery, political, and even romance movies. Ray thus provides your students with a clear, accessible paradigm for interpreting characters from almost any film. Students should have little trouble identifying the paradigm, but be sure, in class, to review the ideological significance of the two character types — a more abstract point that students may overlook. Ask, for instance, why Americans tend to prefer the outlaw hero. What does that reveal about the American character? To encourage students to consider the significance of Ray's categories, we strongly suggest that you do Reading the Signs question 3, which asks the class to brainstorm examples of outlaw and official heroes, then to categorize them according to shared traits (such as race or gender). Consider as well assigning William Martin-Doyle's "*Cool Hand Luke*: The Exclusion of the Official Hero in American Cinema" (p. 36), one of the student essays in the Writing about Popular Culture section. Although not all students will be familiar with *Cool Hand Luke*, Martin-Doyle provides a sufficient summary and uses Ray effectively to interpret the film.

Ray's selection provides an ideal framework for analyzing not only films but other media. Not all heroes need be real, of course; question 1 has students consult Gary Engle's and Andy Medhurst's selections in Chapter Nine and consider which type of hero Superman and Batman are to their audiences (for a simpler question, ask students to analyze just one hero). Questions 2 and 4 are similar, asking students to apply Ray's paradigm to the central characters in the *Terminator* and *Alien* films, respectively; in discussing the *Alien* films, students should consider gender issues as well, for the protagonist is female, and American heroes traditionally have been male. Finally, question 5 is speculative, asking students to create a third category of hero to accommodate the characters in such cartoons as *The Simpsons* and *South Park*. To prepare students for writing about this topic, you might assign the introduction to Chapter Nine, "American Icons: The Mythic Characters of Popular Culture."

LINDA SEGER
CREATING THE MYTH (p. 316)

You'll find that you use Seger's selection clear, accessible discussion in a number of ways. This essay can introduce your students to cultural myths; it provides a critical framework for analyzing a broad range of films; its central argument, that successful films employ archetypes which tap into universal human desires, is open to debate and modification. This essay complements Ray's in that Seger focuses on heroic myths, but unlike Ray she traces classic hero patterns through a single film, *Star Wars*, that should be familiar to most students (be sure to draw their attention to the *Star Wars* photo on p. 318). She also complicates the heroic myth by examining what she calls "broken" characters and combination myths; this examination will give you great flexibility in class discussion, as most films fit her scheme somehow. Seger also raises some interesting open-ended questions (for instance, why the *Rambo* films were so successful). Herself a screenwriter, Seger wrote this selection for a readership of aspiring screenwriters, and that shapes her tone and attitudes. Her status as an industry insider helps to explain her apparent endorsement of using existing myths in film — she doesn't recommend originality in screenplays. You may want to discuss that essentially conservative viewpoint with your class. (Reading the Signs question 1 addresses this issue; question 5 calls for an evaluation of Seger's suggestion that screenwriters use Grimm's fairy tales for inspiration.)

If you're covering both the Ray and the Seger selections, consider assigning question 2, which calls for a gender-based comparison of the two approaches to heroes. Question 3 sends students to Michael Parenti's essay for help in analyzing *Pretty Woman* and *Indecent Proposal*, while question 4 asks them to examine the archetype-filled *Titanic*. Perhaps the most challenging question (and our favorite) is the last, which asks students to explore the myths about American history, race, and gender underlying *Gone with the Wind*. (Remember: The film runs more than three hours and thus is difficult to show in class.) After doing this assignment, some of our students have lamented that they will never view the movie the same way again — proof to us that the assignment works.

GARY JOHNSON
THE WESTERN (p. 326)

In focusing on the iconography of the Western, Johnson's selection is ideal paired with the Ray or the Seger selections in this chapter. Your students may not be fans of this film genre, but see that as an advantage. Because they won't be tempted to champion their favorite movies or stars, students may be more inclined to adopt a critical perspective. You might begin discussion by asking the class to brainstorm all associations they have with Westerns; then turn to Johnson and compare his discussion with your students' list. It's likely that there will be considerable overlap, and you could discuss why, in an era when Westerns have fallen out of cinematic favor, students are so familiar with the conventions. You could also ask students to consider why the Western was so dominant in the early part of the twentieth century. What myths and ideologies did it presume? How might those cultural values have changed, and along with them, the popularity of the genre? Given that some students may not have seen many Westerns, you might rent a few of the classic Westerns that Johnson names and show selected archetypically rich scenes in class; ask whether some of Johnson's broader assertions, such as the claim that John Wayne serves as "a metaphor for America itself," are borne out by the scenes. Direct students' attention to the photo of Clint Eastwood in *Fistful of Dollars* (p. 330): Does Eastwood exemplify any of the character traits that Johnson describes? Alternatively, you might show in class or put on reserve in your school's film library one of the more recent Westerns, such as *Dances with Wolves* or *Unforgiven*. To what extent does the film replicate — or ring changes on — the classic Western iconography?

This selection lends itself to assignments that ask students to interpret particular films. Reading the Signs question 1 sends them to Ray's "The Thematic Paradigm" for help in analyzing the hero of a Western of their choice; alternatively, you can assign students to write about a film that you select and show in class. Students who prefer more contemporary movies might enjoy question 3, which has them interpret a recent Western, *Wild, Wild West*; the film's box-office failure is particularly interesting given the star value of its lead, Will Smith. This question prompts students to consider both the evolution of the genre's popularity and the conventions governing ethnic roles in Westerns. A focused analytic question, number 4 invites students to critique one of Johnson's explanations for the Western's appeal; the broadest, and perhaps most challenging, question is number 2, which asks students to account for the Western's fading popularity at the box office. Be sure they realize that, thanks to video and DVD, Westerns do retain an audience; students might do some Internet research to determine the profile of Western fans, and their results might push them to consider the generational complexities of movie audiences.

SUSAN BORDO

BRAVEHEART, BABE, AND THE CONTEMPORARY BODY (p. 333)

We like Bordo's selection because it provides an excellent analysis of the cultural beliefs that underlie the success of a film like *Braveheart*, beliefs that she sees as dramatically different than those that animate a movie like *Babe*. Bordo masterfully blends discussion of the film with details drawn from the larger cultural system in which it exists, including advertising, the 1996 Summer Olympics, and the fitness industry. That might sound like the essay is diffuse and rambling, but it's anything but that: throughout, Bordo maintains a steady focus on how what she calls the Just-Do-It philosophy dominates both personal self-image and pop culture products. Your students should have little trouble understanding her, but expect some resistance to her critique of the Just-Do-It philosophy. They may ask, what's wrong with self-reliance? Send your students back to Bordo for an answer: she doesn't oppose self-reliance but finds the ideology of success and empowerment to be a deceptive distortion of real-life struggles. (Reading the Signs question 1 allows students to reflect on the influence this philosophy has had on their own lives.) In addition, you might want to direct your students' attention to Bordo's style. Although this is an academic piece, Bordo allows her personal voice to emerge (note the frequent use of the first person and occasional autobiographical details), displays a sense of humor, and moves gracefully and seamlessly from one concrete detail to the next — a good model for students addicted to stuffy academese to emulate.

You'll find that this selection creates opportunities for a creative variety of analytic and argumentative essays. A natural choice would be to ask students to argue for or against Bordo's interpretation of either *Braveheart* or *Babe*. Question 2 invites the class to extend Bordo's analysis to current films; we predict that your students will find that those reflecting the *Braveheart* ideology will outnumber those in the *Babe* vein. The more challenging questions are the last two. Number 3 has students respond to Bordo's criticism of power feminism; you could make this a research topic, with students investigating further this brand of feminism. Finally, number 4 asks students to apply Bordo's argument to an episode of a television talk show; as preparation for this topic, you might assign as well the Steven D. Stark essay on Oprah Winfrey in Chapter Three.

TODD BOYD
So You Wanna Be a Gangsta? (p. 343)

This selection is essential if your course emphasizes ethnic issues; it's also ideal if you like to emphasize the historical context in which pop culture products should be interpreted. Boyd outlines a full and rich history of the gangster genre of film, starting with the good, old-fashioned American Western, moving to ethnic white gangster films such as the *Godfather* series and then the Blaxploitation flicks, and concluding with analyses of *American Me* and *Boyz N the Hood*. You'll find that this historical approach can head off simple evaluative judgments of recent black gangsta films and help prevent unproductive digressions into social issues that are only tangentially related (whether gangsters face a bum rap by society, for instance). Even though both *American Me* and *Boyz N the Hood* are now quite a few years old, we find most first-year students have seen at least one (usually *Boyz*) and often both. Students sometimes see *Boyz* as an "alternative" film; expect some to bristle at Boyd's suggestion that the film reflects a "bourgeois sense of politics." Boyd's writing should be accessible to most students; the one section that may be more difficult is his discussion of black nationalist politics. Determine early in class discussion whether students grasp Boyd's point, since missing it can mean missing his overall argument about *Boyz*.

If you assign this selection, try to arrange an in-class viewing of *Boyz* or place it and *American Me* on reserve in your college's media library: that will allow for a richer discussion of Boyd's readings of these films. A natural assignment based on Boyd's essay is to ask students to view one of the films and either respond to his argument about it or write their own interpretations of it. For a somewhat more complicated topic, try Reading the Signs question 2, which invites students to compare the representation of ethnic "others" in a film such as *Scarface* with that of black gang members in a movie like *Boyz N the Hood*. Two questions allow students to explore the implications raised in Boyd's essay: number 1 asks whether Hollywood glorifies criminal behavior (if you're interested in this angle, you could assign Vivian C. Sobchack's "The Postmorbid Condition" in this chapter as a companion piece), and number 4 asks whether gangsta films exploit the black community. Both questions would make good research paper topics. Question 3 asks students to consider why gangsta culture is so popular among middle-class teens; you could organize your class into teams and have them interview adolescents as a means of gathering primary evidence for their papers. Finally, question 5 extends the issues to gender by asking students to interpret a film that Boyd does not address, *Waiting to Exhale*. Boyd focuses largely on films that feature the black male underclass; you may find it useful to have your students interpret a film with African American characters who are both female and middle-class — a departure from usual cinematic conventions.

JESSICA HAGEDORN
Asian Women in Film: No Joy, No Luck (p. 355)

Hagedorn's selection fits well into courses that focus on either gender or ethnic issues. Although you're not likely to be surprised by her argument — that films tend to relegate Asian women to the traditional whore/angel dichotomy — your students may not have considered this issue at all. If you've read Sandra Tsing Loh's selection in this chapter, you could ask your students to relate the dichotomy Hagedorn describes to Loh's taxonomy of "good " and "bad" girls — the two authors are basically talking about the same gender steretotypes, though Hagedorn adds a racial spin to her treatment of them (see Reading the Signs question 4). Ask them as well to interpret the photos of Michelle Yeoh (p. 357) and Anna May Wong (p. 361): To what extent do these actresses illustrate Hagedorn's point? (Yeoh is best known as Jackie Chan's costar in *Supercop*, and in this photo she plays a Chinese secret agent in *Tomorrow Never Dies*; Wong was an early twentieth-century actress who appeared in *The Thief of Baghdad* [1924] and played a prostitute in *Shanghai Express* [1932].) We should warn you that students may be unhappy with Hagedorn's criticism of *The Joy Luck Club*, a film that we've discovered is a sentimental favorite among many students, both male and female and of all ethnic backgrounds. Since many students have seen this film, you might want to combine your discussion of this essay with a viewing of the film, to allow your students to test Hagedorn's thesis (see Reading the Signs question 1).

A basic analysis assignment is to ask students to view one of the films that Hagedorn mentions (or any other with Asian characters) and interpret the depiction of women in the film. Question 5 is similar, but it has students focus on one of the gender-bending films, such as *M. Butterfly*, that Hagedorn mentions (note that some conservative students may feel uncomfortable watching this film). You can broaden the issues that Hagedorn raises by addressing more generally Hollywood's tendency to stereotype different ethnicities. Question 2 invites the class to stage a debate on this issue; students could prepare for the debate by reading Michael Omi's essay in Chapter Seven. These issues apply to other media as well; question 3 invites students to analyze a magazine that targets Asian American readers. As an alternative to an essay assignment, consider bringing to class some such magazine for small groups to study.

SANDRA TSING LOH
The Return of Doris Day (p. 365)

If your class is emphasizing gender issues, this selection will make a lively and relevant addition to your syllabus. Loh provides a taxonomy of female archetypes in American film (and in popular culture more broadly), arguing that in the mid-1990s the "good girl" archetype triumphed over the "bad girl." You might begin your discussion of this selection by asking your students to complete Reading the Signs question 1, which asks them to explore in a journal entry the extent to which the gender archetypes Loh describes affected them in their childhood. This question should prompt students to consider how traditional gender roles have shaped their own attitudes and beliefs. In addition, Loh's taxonomy creates lots of opportunities for in-class activities. You could have students brainstorm their own updated list of good and bad girls in film, and then explain whatever trends they happen to find (see Reading the Signs question 2). Or ask them to trace in detail the career of one of the figures Loh mentions: Has this figure evolved? If so, how, and, more important, why? For a different perspective, apply Loh's thesis to male characters: Do your students find a predominance of good or bad boys? And what's the significance of their findings? As you discuss this selection, be sure students move from slotting characters and stars into Loh's pigeonholes to contemplating the larger significance of the patterns that they find. (Question 3 urges students to consider the reasons for these patterns.)

Your students will have little trouble understanding this selection, but be aware that Loh's style is decidedly nonacademic. You could discuss her style directly, asking your students what Loh gains — and perhaps loses — by writing in such a resolutely tongue-in-cheek manner. Because Loh provides a paradigm for studying gender roles, this selection is ideal for interpreting particular examples from the media. Questions 4, 5, and 6 ask students to use Loh's essay in analyzing "progressive" TV shows, a Doris Day film, and a women's fashion magazine, respectively. But you can tailor the question to your students' interests by asking them to focus on any film, show, or other media text in which female characters play a significant role.

MICHAEL PARENTI
CLASS AND VIRTUE (p. 373)

We decided to include this selection after hearing the umpteenth student proclaim that *Pretty Woman* is her favorite movie of all time. At least in our classes, most of the film's avid fans have been female — and, to our surprise, most consider themselves feminists. Such students are likely to be irked by Parenti, who finds the film objectionable on many grounds. He concentrates on the class issues implicit in this film and in others; we've found it interesting that many students respond, "Well, of course, one has to get of rid of low-class habits." And we've had students argue that the film doesn't really show prostitution because the rich guy is Prince Charming. The film's fans will relish responding to Reading the Signs question 3, which invites them to argue with Parenti's interpretation. Be sure your students ask "why are we shown *this* ?" when offering a counterinterpretation. Parenti mentions briefly the gender bigotry in the film; question 4 sends students to Holly Devor's essay in Chapter Six for help in analyzing the film's gender roles.

Parenti's comments about class can be applied to examples from other media. It works well when applied to other films such as *Wall Street* (see question 1) or to television shows such as *Beverly Hills 90210* (see question 2); it can also be used to illuminate films such as *On the Waterfront* (see question 5). An exploratory topic, question 6 asks students to create a category of "racial bigotry" to parallel Parenti's two categories of class and gender bigotry. For this question, we strongly suggest that students first read Michael Omi's "In Living Color" (Chapter Seven); Omi comments on the ways the media reinforce ethnic biases.

VIVIAN C. SOBCHACK
The Postmorbid Condition (p. 377)

We like Sobchack's selection because she offers a cultural explanation for the current spate of violent films — a fresh angle that goes beyond the usual debate of the effect of media violence on our culture. Her writing is accessible but on the theoretical side, so you might want to walk your students through her essay. She begins by describing succinctly an article she had written twenty-five years earlier on violence in film; at that time, she saw the violence as being aestheticized. To demonstrate what she means by this, you might show in class a short clip from *Bonnie and Clyde* or another film from the era. Then your students will be better prepared for her indictment of more recent violent movies, ones that she feels do quite the opposite: rather than aestheticizing violence, she claims, current films are "careless" about it. The blasted bodies are just that, bodies, not people; the technologizing and escalation of violence becomes the object of interest, not pain and suffering; and the violence becomes an illusory joke, not a moral offense. While she finds the depiction of modern culture as postmodern to be tiresome, nonetheless you might get your class to appreciate the connotations of her title, for "postmorbid" echoes *postmodern*, and she essentially is critiquing a postmodern tendency to substitute image and effect for substance and the real. A effective way to get to the heart of her essay is to tease out the reasons she distinguishes overtly violent films like *Saving Private Ryan* and *Beloved* from overtly violent films like *Pulp Fiction* and *Reservoir Dogs*. Ask your students how they responded to the violent scenes in the first two films: Did they laugh? Or did they squirm, turn their heads, or feel disgusted? If the latter, that's because the violence is made to seem real and carries with it a moral burden. It's likely students didn't react that way watching the second pair of films, because, as Sobchack points out, the violence is hyperbolic and over the top. And that, she finds, is exactly what's wrong with it. Students might analyze the poster for *Reservoir Dogs* (p. 383) to analyze what sort of violence it depicts.

Once students grasp her point, they're likely to want to debate it. Many students have grown up watching violent films and may see nothing wrong with unreal violence; in fact, they may argue that it's superior in that everyone knows it's "just entertainment." You might ask your class what that says about cultural values and attitudes. Reading the Signs question 6 invites the class to discuss this issue, though you could make it an essay topic; the next selection in the chapter, Patrick Goldstein's "The Time to Get Serious Has Come," can shed some light on this matter as well. You might also get your students to talk about the gendered patterns of responding to violent movies (in an aside, Sobchack points out that fans of cinematic violence tend to be male). In writing on this essay, students would do well to ground their arguments in specific examples of violent films. Question 4 has them do so by testing Sobchack's claim on a recent movie (of course, you could select one of those that she discusses as well), while question 2 invites them to take on her argument about why films like Beloved were disappointments at the box office. Sobchack doesn't directly discuss gangster films, which also are quite violent; a challenging question, number 5 asks students to argue whether the violence in a film like Boyz N the Hood is desensitizing or real. Finally, questions 1 and 3 ask students address broader issues of the effects of violence on audiences and of the possible need for restrictions of violence; if you assign these questions, you might first have the class brainstorm films that would provide relevant evidence for their arguments, no matter what position they take.

PATRICK GOLDSTEIN
THE TIME TO GET SERIOUS HAS COME (p. 384)

After the September 11 attacks, many a media pundit proclaimed that American media, particularly TV and film, would have to change their casual depiction of international violence and horrors, for no longer could audiences see hijackings and bombings as just entertainment. Patrick Goldstein would wish the same result — but he's skeptical about whether such a change will indeed happen, pointing to recent changes as being "cosmetic." What's useful about his piece is his grounding of this question within the context of cinematic history, looking at post–World War II and late 1960s responses to contemporary events. Ask your students what the cultural mood of those eras was (the answer is implicit in Goldstein's essay) and how that mood might have shaped cinematographers' creations. Then ask them about the mood before — and after — the 9/11 attacks: How might the nation's shock, resurgence of patriotism, and exhortations to "just get on with life" affected post-9/11 filmmaking? (Reading the Signs question 1 asks them to address this question, while question 4 has them analyze the cultural mood of one decade, the 1990s.) Since students have the benefit of hindsight that Goldstein didn't have (his article was published September 18, 2001), encourage them to refer to specific recent films as they discuss and write about this essay.

Goldstein's selection is ideal if you wish your students to consider the ethical dimensions of American popular culture. Reading the Signs question 2 has them take on the debatable question of whether films like *Collateral Damage* ever should have been released, while number 3 has them argue about Hollywood's abandonment of real-life issues (Tom Shales's "Resisting the False Security of TV" in Chapter Three could be a useful supplementary essay to assign for this topic). For both of these questions, students might want to research the box-office response to post–9/11 releases that went ahead anyway and showed as entertaining what many in real life found to be anything but.

PART TWO
Cultural Constructions

Chapter Five
POPULAR SPACES
Interpreting the Built Environment

If you want your students to enjoy the intellectual pleasure of analyzing something they probably have never studied in school, this chapter's for you. This chapter is among our favorites, because we've found that our students approach writing essays on both domestic and public places with incredible enthusiasm and zeal. If you're emphasizing the semiotic method, this chapter can help overcome any resistance you face among students who bristle, say, at interpreting their favorite film because they identify too closely with it. Students tend to feel less personally attached to the built environment (particularly to public spaces) and thus may find it easier to attain critical distance from the objects of their analysis. And there's plenty to analyze: buildings aren't just brick or stucco or glass; they are rich sign systems that define power structures and hierarchies (it was no accident that the September 11 attacks targeted edifices that symbolized American economic supremacy and military might), control visitors' behavior, and establish territorial boundaries. As the Discussing the Signs of Public Space boxed question suggests, you might start discussion with your own classroom: are chairs arranged in neat rows or in a circle, and how does the arrangement affect class dynamics? Are chairs bolted to the floor, and if so, what are the implications for pedagogical style? What sort of hierarchy is implied in the traditional lecture hall? You can extend this discussion to other parts of the campus: In which buildings do students feel more comfortable, and why? What messages are sent by your school's architecture? Ask your students to check your school's Web site to learn which buildings are featured: Why are *these* buildings and not others used to represent the campus? To stimulate your students' curiosity, assign the Exploring the Signs of Public Space boxed question, which has students reflect on their own use of public space for recreation or entertainment. Students taken by this topic might enjoy as well the Reading the Signs of Virtual Space on the Net boxed question, which asks them to consider how "virtual" space may alter our understanding and experience of space. You might pair this question with an analysis of the home-as-work-space photo on p. 394. In what ways does our increasing reliance on the Internet for business, research, and entertainment affect domestic relationships?

You'll see that many of the questions that accompany the readings in this chapter call for a kind of field research — that is, they ask students to visit a public place and analyze it. If you give such an assignment, you'll want to ascertain that your students have an equal ability to get to the place (it wouldn't be fair to expect students to drive fifty miles to an amusement park, for instance, especially when some may not have a car) and that the place is appropriate (we once counseled a novice instructor *not* to suggest a strip club as an assignment option). Since students may not have experience doing this sort of field research, you might spend some class time discussing note-taking techniques and observational strategies. We've found it useful to prepare observational guidelines with questions that help focus students' attention on important details. For instance, someone studying a public park might respond to questions such as "Are visitors primarily alone, in pairs, in large groups? Do people who seem to be strangers interact with each other? Do visitors walk slowly or quickly? Do they linger

POPULAR SPACES

and relax? What is it about the physical design of the park that encourages this behavior?" Note that such assignments are ideal for small group projects and observational teams: Students may simply *see* more if they are with others, and they'll enjoy the camaraderie of the shared experience.

If you can't cover the entire chapter, we suggest you start with the introduction, which establishes a critical framework for analyzing public space, and then pick selections according to the type of space analyzed or the issues raised. Commerical and entertainment spaces are analyzed in the Susan Willis (Disney World), Anna McCarthy (NikeTown), and the Malcolm Gladwell (retail stores) selections. Lucy R. Lippard and Daphne Spain both address the gendered implications of architectural design, with Lippard considering urban space and Spain emphasizing the modern office environment. The Lippard piece also complements Camilo José Vergara's selection on the city itself as a space. For a first-person account of the dynamics of domestic space, assign Karen Karbo's "The Dining Room." Rina Swentzell examines the cultural values implicit in architecture in her comparision of Native American and mainstream school design. Finally, Eric Boehlert closes the chapter with a historical reading of the World Trade Center, a group of buildings that continues to demonstrate the enduring symbolic power of public space long after the rubble has been hauled away.

MALCOLM GLADWELL
The Science of Shopping (p. 403)

We've chosen to lead off the chapter with Gladwell's essay because we find students respond passionately to it. And you can have a lot of fun with this piece. It's a detailed description of the ways retailers use spatial design to manipulate consumers and to stimulate the urge to buy. Whether your students are city folk or suburbanites, well-off or struggling to make ends meet, you can assume that they're familiar with some sort of mall and that their consuming behavior has been affected by the mall's design. Thus this selection provides a good opportunity for combining discussion of personal experience with an analysis of a topic accessible to all students. Some students may resist the notion that one's behavior can be shaped by architecture and physical clues, but remind them that this is the assumption that successful retailers make: It's not just Gladwell's opinion. Indeed, Gladwell focuses his essay on Paco Underhill, a sort of retailers' anthropologist who studies consumer behavior. If students don't believe that Underhill's advice to retailers would have an effect, ask them to consider alternatives: If a huge shopping mall didn't have a food court, would shoppers behave in the same way? Why do college bookstores locate popular trade books, bestsellers, and merchandise such as calendars up front, near the cash registers, with the required textbooks relegated to the back? Have your students ever bought an unnecessary gee-gaw because of this arrangement? For more on Underhill's strategies, consult the Web site for Envirosell, his behavioral market research and consulting company (**www.envirosell.com**).

In varying ways, the Reading the Signs questions ask students to apply or respond to Gladwell's observations about the science behind customer manipulation. Question 1 invites students to respond to Gladwell's question, "Should we be afraid of Paco Underhill?" Be sure students note that, while at times Gladwell seems to suggest that his answer is yes, ultimately he decides that it is the shoppers who manipulate the retailers — a debatable point given his evidence. Two questions ask students to apply Gladwell's points to specific examples: Number 2 has them visit a local store (it could be one that Gladwell mentions, such as Banana Republic) or supermarket, and number 4 has them visit the Web site of a major retailer and study how the virtual space encourages them to buy. This topic is the more challenging of the two, for students may see some features of the Web site as mere functional conveniences (e.g., the "shopping carts" that allow you to pile up merchandise as you're "browsing" through the store), though, while they may be helpful to the virtual shopper, also stimulate additional consumption (it's easy to forget how much you've stashed in your cart). Your students may be disturbed by the invasion of personal privacy that's implicit in some of Paco Underhill's techniques; if that's the case, they may enjoy the class debate suggested in question 3 on the ethics of retail anthropology (Eric Schlosser's "Kid Kustomers" in Chapter Two could provide supplementary information for this topic).

ANNA MCCARTHY
BRAND IDENTITY AT NIKETOWN (p. 410)

Your students don't have to be familiar with a NikeTown outlet in order to appreciate this selection. Not only does McCarthy describe a sample outlet thoroughly; she offers ample comparison with other instances of supposed postmodern "shoppertainment." Your students will be familiar with the various in-store promotions, videos, and visual techniques that are so ubiquitous now, especially in stores that target the youth market; however, they may need a little help in grasping the subtleties of her argument. Be sure to ask them what she means by claiming that NikeTown's in-store marketing strategies produce a sense of disorientation. Why would a store, a brand name, want to establish a depersonalized relationship with its consumers? How does this strategy work to create a sense of mystique for the product line? Ask students as well about the image they associate with Nike products. What attitude does it convey? And how does that image influence consumer behavior, particularly for a product line (athletic shoes) that is competing in an oversaturated market (dozens of shoe companies manufacture hundreds of models).

A classic essay assignment (Reading the Signs number 2) asks students to visit a NikeTown and to write their own analysis of the outlet's in-store marketing techniques. Does McCarthy's critique still apply, or has NikeTown altered its strategies? If so, to what end? If a NikeTown is not located in your community, ask students to visit a retail outlet that employs similar layout and video displays. Or students could visit a single-brand store, such as Warner Bros. or Disney, that also sells a corporate and a brand image along with the products. The question suggests that students consult Gladwell's "The Signs of Shopping"; be sure students grasp that the disorienting effects of NikeTown displays are rather different than those engineered by Paco Underhill. To prepare students for a visit to a retail outlet, assign question number 3, which asks the class to brainstorm companies that promote brand image as a commodity (consider listing on the board all the items of clothing worn by your students that prominently display brand logos — the results may be amusing!). For argumentative topics, consider assigning question 1, which asks students to apply Kalle Lasn's strident critique of advertising from Chapter Two to NikeTown, or question 4, which has them take on McCarthy's assertion that NikeTown's marketing techniques are "Orwellian." This last question could also serve as the basis of an in-class debate about the effects and the ethics of modern marketing techniques.

SUSAN WILLIS
DISNEY WORLD: PUBLIC USE/PRIVATE STATE (p. 415)

Willis's essay is one of the more difficult in this book, and you may want to spend some time discussing critical reading strategies. You could ask students to outline her essay in their journals or to jot down a list of unfamiliar terms as they read and to propose, in their own words, definitions of those terms. Ask them to identify the argument and the wealth of support Willis offers (though occasionally abstract, this article is filled with specific details and anecdotes that students should have little trouble understanding). The Reading the Text questions all focus on Willis's main points, so you might also assign those questions as a reading log.

This selection is well worth the effort students may need to expend, however. Willis turns to a significant category of the built environment — the artificial world created by theme parks such as Disney World — and analyzes how the park's design encourages consumption. Be prepared for some resistance to her thesis: students often cling to childhood favorites, equating an analysis of them to an attack on themselves. If they do so, be sure to ask them the ever-useful question "Why?" Why did Disneyland, in a different venue, come up with "Disney Dollars"? Why don't we see kids playing spontaneously at Disney World? And make sure they don't rest content with the easy answer "Disney World is just fun." (Skeptical students may appreciate it if you assign Reading the Signs question 2, which invites students to support or refute one of Willis's central contentions.) If your students are unfamiliar with Disney World, ask them to apply her thesis to a local theme park they may have visited (see question 3). Although Willis focuses on Disney World, her argument extends to other theme parks and consumer products. Question 1 asks students to consider a related phenomenon, the plethora of Disney products, characters, and movies (here, too, expect a few students to defend Disney as if the company were equivalent to their own identity — a real sign of Disney's impact). A more challenging topic, number 5 calls for a comparison of the ways Disney World and a local shopping mall control spending behavior. Students will be prepared for this question if they read Anne Norton's "The Signs of Shopping" or Rachel Bowlby's "The Haunted Superstore" in Chapter One and Malcolm Gladwell's "The Science of Shopping" in this chapter. The question that demands the most creativity is 4, which asks students to design a theme park for the twenty-first century. As part of this question, ask students to articulate the rationale behind their design choices — a sure way to encourage them to see the ideological underpinnings of something so seemingly innocent as a child's fantasyland.

LUCY R. LIPPARD
ALTERNATING CURRENTS (p. 427)

We felt a chapter on the built environment practically required a discussion of the city and the country, and Lippard's selection fits the bill beautifully. The "alternating current" of her title is the push-pull that most Americans feel, at one time or another, between the high energy and drama of the city and the calming influence of a rural area. What we like about this selection is that Lippard goes beyond simply describing this dynamic to explore the symbolic (and semiotic) significances of each context, explaining, for instance, both the positive and negative associations attached to cities.

(Note that Lippard focuses more on cities and that her comments on the country are briefer and more implicit.) Before your students read this selection, ask them to brainstorm associations they have with the country and the city, then have them compare their results with the attributes Lippard describes. They may be interested in seeing how many of their prior attitudes are included in her discussion — and in recognizing that their own beliefs can fit into a full intellectual context. And encourage your students to relate their own experiences in different environments to Lippard's points. If your students are attending an urban college away from home, for instance, ask them to relate their experience of moving to school to Lippard's comments about the ways cities affect newcomers. If you're emphasizing gender issues, the Lippard article can be useful as well because she makes some debatable claims about what the city can represent to women in particular (Reading the Signs question 5 asks students to evaluate the validity of Lippard's gender-related claims). Question 1 is a journal topic that asks students to reflect on whether they have felt the alternating current that Lippard describes. Because some students may have lived in the same place all their lives, or because some may not be independent enough to see themselves as having options for where to live, you might encourage them to view this prompt broadly: Do they long for a camping vacation in the summer? How does a week-long wilderness hike make them feel? Lippard's focus on the binary poles of country and city largely excludes an environment that may in fact be more typical of where Americans live, the suburbs; thus, question 2 invites students to analyze the suburb's mythological significance. For focused questions that require students to handle specific evidence, consider assigning question 3, which invites them to conduct a survey on why urbanites are "lured" by their environment, and question 4, which asks students to test one of Lippard's claims about urban or rural landmarks.

KAREN KARBO

The Dining Room (p. 434)

Expect your students — both male and female, young and older — to feel deeply moved by Karbo's selection. A memoir, this piece is a coming-of-age tale that charts Karbo's shifting relationship with her family, particularly with her mother; the changes in their relationship are paralleled by changes in the family's dining rooms as they move from house to house. Indeed, the dining rooms not only represent the family dynamic but also work to control it. This selection is ideal for discussing the often unrecognized influence of domestic space: ask your students to reflect on the ways their own homes' design affects family interactions. Do they have "neutral" space, where family members enjoy equal status? Or are some rooms marked as territory for one person? What happens if territorial boundaries are transgressed? You can develop this discussion by studying the photo of the father and son arguing at dinner on p. 442. What signs indicate that the characters are related, and what seems to be the dynamic among them? Beyond raising the issue of domestic space, this selection also is well-suited for teaching close reading techniques. Be sure to discuss Karbo's use of the second person: Why would a memoir writer elect this form of address, and what effect does it have on the reader? Ask students to pay attention to stylistic details as well. Why does Karbo capitalize some words, such as Special Occasion and Fancy, that normally are not capitalized? How does the capitalization work to create an image of Karbo's mother? One reason students find this selection engaging, we believe, is Karbo's subtle sense of humor. What makes some of the passages humorous, and why do students think Karbo includes humor in a tale that has a sad conclusion?

"The Dining Room" lends itself to both straightforward analytic essays and to more imaginative assignments. Reading the Signs question 1 has students analyze the ways the various dining tables and rooms symbolically represent Karbo's relationship with her mother; for a close textual analysis, assign question 4, which focuses on Karbo's characterization of her mother. For a more personal response, question 3 invites students to write their own memoir of a significant physical space; the question can be reformulated into an analytic essay if you prefer. Question 4 requires the most creativity, because it asks students to assume the role of Karbo's mother and to write her remembrance of the dining rooms the selection describes. To prepare students for this topic, you might discuss in class the dynamics among all the family members: What role does Karbo's father play? Why do we see so little of him? And what sort of relationship exists between Karbo's parents?

DAPHNE SPAIN

Spatial Segregation and Gender Stratification in the Workplace (p. 443)

This selection is perfect for addressing the ways in which the built environment can replicate cultural gender norms. Although the style of this selection is a tad dry, your students should find it easy to grasp Spain's main ideas about the gendered patterns in contemporary office environments. Be sure they focus on her distinction between "open floor" and "closed door," and encourage them to articulate the power relations that are implied by each type of office design. Ask them about their own experiences in work environments. Whether male or female, they most likely have occupied lower-level or intern positions and thus probably have experienced the hierarchical arrangements enforced by design. Why is a view office considered a sign of importance? Why, in the aftermath of John F. Kennedy Jr.'s death in 1999, did so many commentators note how remarkable it was that his office at *George* magazine was located on the same floor as those of the staffers? Then you can move to Spain's argument about gender stratification; you might note that, while women have moved into higher corporate spheres, the general patterns of employment that she describes still dominate the workplace.

Students should enjoy testing Spain's ideas on work environments with which they are familiar. Reading the Signs question 2 has students analyze the office where they work; as an alternative, students could study a staff office or even faculty offices at your college. For a topic that requires students to conduct interviews, assign question 3, which focuses on Spain's contention about the nature of women's work. An imaginative topic, question 1 invites students to work in groups to design a nonhierarchical office space. We suggest that you have each group present their proposal to the class, briefly outlining the rationale for their design. Your students can have some fun with question 4, which has them write a hypothetical response to the "ideal" boss-secretary relationship that Spain quotes in this selection. Expect a wide range of responses, especially in this post-Enron, post-Worldcom era, to the notion that the purpose of a secretarial job is to serve as custodian for the boss's "secrets."

RINA SWENTZELL

Conflicting Landscape Values: The Santa Clara Pueblo and Day School (p. 450)

The first time we assigned this selection, we weren't sure whether our students, who are mostly urban Californians, would relate to Swentzell's topic. Our concerns proved baseless, however, as students seemed fascinated not only by Swentzell's comparison of Native American and mainstream worldviews but also by her discussion of the way a school's architectural design can embody a particular educational philosophy. Swentzell's writing is clear and accessible. You might organize your class discussion around the two worldviews that she describes. Ask students to brainstorm on the board the cultural values implicit in the Pueblo culture, for instance, and then to list the physical and architectural features common to traditional Pueblo communities. How do those features perpetuate traditional values? What approach to education and learning do they encourage? Then do the same for the Bureau of Indian Affairs school. What are the design features of this school, and what cultural and social values does it promote? What sort of pedagogy does the design dictate? Such questions can lead to a discussion of larger political issues as students consider the relation between the built environment, cultural dominance, and political power.

This selection can stimulate students to consider their own educational environment and the pedagogy that it encourages. We urge you to assign Reading the Signs question 1, which asks the class to analyze the design of your composition classroom (you could make this either a discussion topic or an essay assignment). Alternatively, students could compare two different sorts of classrooms — a lecture hall and a seminar room, for instance — addressing not only their physical layout but also the style of learning that each allows. We've created two questions that address the ideologies underlying school architectual design. Question 2 asks students to analyze the BIA Day School as a reflection of the myth of a manifest destiny, and question 3 sends them to Fan Shen's "The Classroom and the Wider Culture: Identity as a Key to Learning English Composition" (Chapter 7), prompting them to identify and evaluate the non-Western educational approaches that both authors describe. Question 4 focuses less on design than on pedagogy, inviting the class to debate the merits of hands-on learning at the university level. For this question, be sure that student consider how such learning could occur in a variety of disciplines, including the sciences, the humanities, and the arts.

CAMILO JOSÉ VERGARA

The Ghetto Cityscape (p. 461)

You should find this selection easy to teach, even if your students have little knowledge of the inner city. You might begin discussion by having students brainstorm their impressions of a ghetto environment (preferably before they have read the selection): don't be surprised if their impressions echo those of scholars to whom Vergara alludes early in the piece. Then move to his main point, which is that, rather than being uniform places of ruin, inner city environments can have quite different characters and are not necessarily places of total devastation. Vergara provides a handy paradigm for analyzing such environments; his triad of green ghettos, institutional ghettos, and new immigrant ghettos is accessible and tailor-made for applying to specific urban areas. If you teach in a city, ask your students to analyze it using this framework; if Vergara's categories don't quite fit, challenge students to modify them or to devise their own (see Reading the Signs question 1). Even if you don't teach in a city, this paradigm is still useful, for most suburbs and small towns have their older or relatively impoverished sections that reflect Vergara's distinctions. Indeed, this selection could be valuable in helping students observe spatial detail in any community, not just in the inner city.

This selection pairs well with Lippard's "Alternating Currents," for though these authors share the assumption that a sense of place has a profound effect on human consciousness, their focuses and concerns differ. Reading the Signs question 2 asks students to adopt Vergara's perspective and critique Lippard's reading of the city; alternatively, you could simply ask students to compare and contrast the two writers' views. One issue that emerges in this selection is the role that nature plays in shaping an urban environment; thus, question 3 asks students to explore this role. Note that this can be a rich, complex topic; you might assign the Lippard and the Swentzell selections to help trigger your students' thinking on the matter. If you want your students to do a little reseach, have them investigate the ways in which public parks affect urban life. Perhaps the most challenging topic is number 4, which has students argue for or against Vergara's basic premise that the city's physical environment is at least as influential as economic factors in shaping people's lives.

ERIC BOEHLERT

New York's Most Disliked Building? (p. 467)

We'd guess that most students have vivid memories of watching television on September 11, 2001, and etched in their minds is the terrible collapse of the famous twin towers. Indeed, that awful sight has often been likened to the assassination of John F. Kennedy or, to a lesser extent, the explosion of the space shuttle *Challenger* as an iconic part of cultural memory. You might begin discussion of this selection by discussing the World Trade Center's symbolic significance. How might that significance differ depending on one's perspective as an American? More specifically, as a New Yorker? Or as a militant terrorist? Why was it the target of terrorists, not just in 2001 but also in 1993? As you contemplate this question, study the photo of the WTC on p. 469 and the images of their destruction on pp. 20–23. Ask your students as well to consider the history of the WTC that Boehlert sketches. How was the WTC initially received, both by the public and by the architectural community? How did those responses evolve as the towers came to occupy what at one time seemed to be a permanent, anchoring role in the New York City skyline?

Boehlert's selection is flexible enough to invite assignments that focus either on the World Trade Center itself or on other buildings. Reading the Text question 1 asks students to assess the towers' posthumous symbolic significance; to develop support for their arguments, students could research the on-going debates over whether the towers should be rebuilt and over what sort of memorial would be appropriate for the WTC site. For a more focused topic, question 3 asks students to write an argumentative response to the claim that the WTC was an "arrogant" design. Question 2 extends the issues to your own community, asking students to analyze a local public building that has symbolic status. Beyond visiting the building, students might consult a local library or city hall for archival documents related to the planning and design of the building.

Alternatively, students could select a building that, like the World Trade Center, was initially greeted with skepticism if not outright hostility, and they could research the history of its public reception. Has the building's symbolic significance evolved, and, if so, how can the change be explained? Buildings or monuments that come to mind include the Transamerica pyramid in San Francisco, the Sears tower in Chicago, or the arch in St. Louis.

Chapter Six
WE'VE COME A LONG WAY, MAYBE
Gender Codes in American Culture

If you want your course to focus on one far-ranging theme, you'd do well to select gender as your topic. Not only can students easily see how it shapes their everyday lives, but it affects every area of popular culture. Each chapter in this text has at least one selection that, at least in part, treats gender, so you should have no difficulty identifying a sufficient number of readings to cover a term (see p. 9 of this manual for suggested additional readings from *Signs of Life* for a gender-themed course). We have quite deliberately constructed this chapter to show students that gender is an issue for both women and men, that gender should not be confined to women's studies courses. Occasionally male students quietly — and sometimes not so quietly — tune out when gender becomes a focus in their courses, assuming, as Deborah Tannen points out in her essay, that they are not "marked" by gender as are their female peers. We wish to counter that assumption, for we believe males and females, heterosexuals and homosexuals, are equally subject to our culture's gender norms and mythologies, though the effects can differ radically for each group and for each individual. Accordingly, we treat gender issues broadly in this chapter, addressing both men and women in the chapter's introduction and including readings that explore the signs of both genders.

Assumptions about gender can be deeply rooted, so don't be surprised if your students react spontaneously or even emotionally to the topic. We've found that students usually enjoy discussing gender issues, but for some, just raising them seems to cast doubt on what's "normal." The Exploring the Signs of Gender topic thus is designed to allow students to explore their own assumptions about gender and how these assumptions were shaped. We've found it's most effective to structure class discussion to stimulate lively but controlled conversation about these issues. You can alternate between arranging students in same- and mixed-sex groups, for instance, to take advantage of gender dynamics. You might want to do that with the Discussing the Signs of Gender question, which asks students in small groups to study the gender roles depicted in popular magazines. If you have an ethnically diverse group, asking students to contribute perspectives that differ from "traditional" American gender norms can help show how they are culturally, not biologically, constructed. No matter what your students' backgrounds, we urge you to assume that all students are gender-marked, even if our culture assumes otherwise. We've deliberately made the Reading Gender on the Net exercise broad, inviting them to explore how the Net defines gender issues. If you assign your students this topic, encourage them to read their findings as a sign of what our culture identifies as "male" and "female" concerns.

Holly Devor's selection is essential for its theoretical argument that gender is socially constituted. It provides a framework for understanding the other selections in the chapter, as well as many selections throughout the text. Though one of the text's more difficult selections, it's extremely useful pedagogically. We include Kevin Jennings's memoir about growing up gay and coming to terms with his sexual orientation next, largely to counter the equation between gender and heterosexuality. Another counterpoint is offered by Deborah Blum, who contrasts with Devor in outlining the ways biology affects gender roles and behavior. Blum's piece, which talks about childhood development, can be paired with Jennifer Scanlon's selection, which discusses the ways in which board games socialize young girls to traditional gender norms. Children grow into teens, of course, and Andre Mayer follows by studying the very chauvinistic styles adopted by teen pop culture stars like Britney Spears. Next Naomi Wolf, Deborah Tannen, and James William Gibson address particular signs of gender identity: Wolf focuses on the pressure women face to be extravagantly slender; Tannen argues that women are always "marked" in our society; Gibson surveys popular culture to explain why the warrior has become a model for male identity. The chapter concludes with Laura Miller's selection on gender and cyberspace, which defends the Net against charges of being a mysogynistic environment.

HOLLY DEVOR
GENDER ROLE BEHAVIORS AND ATTITUDES (p. 484)

We highly recomend that you include Holly Devor's essay in your syllabus, for its overview of gender roles and the signs used to communicate them provides a basic critical framework for the chapter's remaining selections. But we warn you: Devor's writing style is somewhat academic and dense, and your students may find it tough going. We suggest that you use the essay as an occasion for discussing critical reading strategies and techniques for comprehending academic writing. You might ask your students to annotate the essay as they read it, and then, in small groups, to review their annotations — and their sense of what Devor's major points are. Or ask them to prepare review questions. At the beginning of class, have students write their questions on the board; you can quickly see which parts of the essay may have been confusing and warrant in-depth discussion.

Despite the difficulty, Devor's essay is well worth the effort. Not only does she chart the traditional cues of "masculinity" and "femininity," but she makes clear how they are cultural constructs, not biological necessities. You'll want to make sure students understand that, when talking about these cues, Devor is describing social norms, not her recommendations for how people should act (students might complain, for instance, that she wants women to be passive — quite the contrary). Her emphasis on social construction thus makes her essay a must-read if you're using a semiotic approach. Students tend not to dispute her general claims about the socially constructed nature of gender, but they do occasionally have trouble with two of her premises. First, they may resist the notion that signs of masculinity carry with them a position of social power and dominance — in other words, that gender norms can have some inequitable consequences. You might address this issue by discussing specific, concrete examples; the Deborah Tannen selection could help in this regard. Second, Devor suggests the possibility of mixing gender norms (the selection is excerpted from her book *Gender Blending*), and this may make some students uncomfortable. If you're game, you could broaden the terms of discussion to include the assumption that heterosexuality is the only morally acceptable sexual preference in America — but be prepared for hearing some strongly entrenched beliefs on this issue.

Because Devor provides a broad theoretical framework for viewing gender, her selection is ideal for applying to specific evidence. Consider doing the first Reading the Signs question in class before discussing the essay; that way you'll be able to refer back to students' presumptions about gender later. The question asks students to brainstorm gender traits in small groups and then to write their lists on the board. If students form same-sex groups, we can guarantee a lively discussion! Even students challenged by Devor's essay should be able to respond to most of the remaining questions. Question 2 allows students to assume the role of sociologist by asking them to use a friend's behavior as evidence they can analyze in terms of gender norms. Question 3 picks up on Devor's comments about body language and sends students to popular magazines to examine the gender-related postures of models (we've found that men in particular are allowed a limited range of postures in ads, with the limitations being greatest in men's magazines such as *GQ*). Finally, question 4 asks students to address the genuinely debatable issue of whether fashion continues to restrict the female body more than the male body.

KEVIN JENNINGS
American Dreams (p. 489)

Kevin Jennings's selection is one of our favorites, and not simply for its clear writing, mild sense of humor, and engaging individual voice. In this personal narrative, Jennings describes how he came to terms with being gay while growing up, combating not normative gender roles but also his own sense of insecurity. In the process, Jennings creates a whole cultural context for understanding why gays and lesbians are so often seen as the "other" in our society; indeed, as he describes his growing desires during adolescence to join the mainstream, to capture the traditional American dream, what emerges are multiple layers of "otherness." First Jennings became aware of geographical otherness and attempted to erase the signs that he was a southerner. What's interesting here is that he became an active participant in maintaining the distinction between mainstream and other (Reading the Signs question 2 asks students to write an essay in which they explore this issue further). What's even more interesting is that Jennings repeats this pattern, for a time, with his sexual orientation. That is, at first he tried to deny his homosexuality to himself, and this effort continued even when Jennings got to college. Note that when Jennings says that by accepting his identity as a gay man he has "done the most American thing of all," he is assuming a different definition of the American dream than the one he assumed in the beginning of the selection. Be sure to ask your students how the dream changes for Jennings thoughout his process of self-discovery. And encourage them to study the photo of the gay rights rally on p. 491. We deliberately include an image of gay senior citizens to counter the more common stereotype, so often projected in media today, of gays as hip and always young.

Although some students may feel that Jennings is a tad sentimental, expect that most students will respond positively to this very open, honest piece. Given the personal nature of this selection, students may enjoy responding to Reading the Signs question 1, a journal topic that has them reflect on the pressures of normative gender roles that they may have felt during their teens. Because both Jennings and Melissa Algranati (Chapter Seven) are young people who narrate their experiences growing up and struggling with their identity, question 4 poses a straightforward comparison and contrast assignment based on their selections. For a challenging argumentative topic, see question 3, which focuses on popular media's role in perpetuating a heterosexual norm. For this topic, be sure students look beyond the occasional media-hyped character or episode (Ellen DeGeneres, for instance, or Roseanne Barr's sharing a kiss with a woman) to consider the typical ways in which gender roles are defined.

DEBORAH BLUM

THE GENDER BLUR: WHERE DOES BIOLOGY END AND SOCIETY TAKE OVER? (p. 495)

As a clear explication of biology's influence on gender behaviors, Deborah Blum's piece serves as a direct response to Holly Devor's claim that gender is a social construct. As Blum herself points out, her argument is not exactly politically correct (readers familiar with the work of writers such as Emily Martin will bristle at her acceptance of the term "default sex" in reference to females). But don't expect her viewpoint to be reactionary: we like her essay precisely because it avoids the simplistic either-or thinking that often dominates the culture-versus-nature debate on gender matters. Indeed, Blum acknowledges that many of our gender codes are cultural constructs; what she argues, however, is that evidence suggests that biology has far more influence on gender behaviors than most humanists want to admit. To academics accustomed to social construction theories, that might seem like an untenable position, but another reason we like this piece is her careful approach to argumentation. In a nice Rogerian style, she begins with a personal anecdote that validates her readership's likely assumptions that gender is only a social construct (this piece originally appeared in the *Utne Reader*) and then explains how her thinking about gender evolved to include biological influence. Ask your students to chart the many ways in which she anticipates her readership's probable responses to her claims. Even though Blum occasionally talks about XX and XY chromosomes and Leydig cell hypoplasia, she is a Pulitzer Prize–winning science writer who knows how to make technical information accessible to the nonspecialist reader. You can use her piece as a model of clarity and specificity sans goopy jargon.

Particularly if you pair this selection with the Holly Devor essay, your students should be well equipped to write argumentative essays. The natural question to accompany this pairing is Reading the Signs question 2, which invites students to respond to Blum's challenge to the social construction view of gender. Because Blum talks a good deal about her own observations as a mother, it's likely your students will want to discuss child-rearing strategies; an imaginative topic, question 2 prompts students to suggest appropriate ways to raise boys given the biological evidence that Blum sets forth. To extend Blum's argument, question 4 invites students to research the current findings on the genetic basis of sexual orientation (recent studies have found that homosexuality may have some genetic influence). To allow students to respond personally to Blum's often personal essay, assign question 1, a journal entry on how one's upbringing affects one's understanding of gender norms.

We encourage you to study in class the photo of the stork and infants with male and females signs sitting in a shopping cart on p. 502. Ask your students: How is the gender of each baby indicated, and why are the babies — and the stork — sitting in a shopping cart? What is the photographer trying to suggest about gender roles in modern American society?

JENNIFER SCANLON

BOYS-R-US: BOARD GAMES AND THE SOCIALIZATION OF YOUNG ADOLESCENT GIRLS (p. 503)

Jennifer Scanlon's essay pairs nicely with Michael A. Messner's selection in Chapter Eight, for just as sports lead boys to adopt traditional male gender roles, the same-sex board games Scanlon describes socialize girls to embrace traditional female roles. We've found that students enjoy talking about their childhood experiences, and given the accessibility of Scanlon's writing, you should have no trouble triggering a lively discussion of this selection. You might start by dividing the board in two sections, one for girls and one for boys, and having the whole class come to the board and, in the appropriate section, identify a favorite toy or game from childhood (asking students to do this en masse will yield more candid responses). Then stand back and look for patterns: To what extent are the toys and games gender-specific? Are gender-neutral toys mentioned, and, if so, are they more common for girls or for boys? You may have some students complain that Scanlon makes "too much" out of games, saying, "I didn't think about these issues as a child." Use these objections as an opportunity to to ask that handy question, "Why *this*?" Why is it that so few gender-neutral toys exist for children? Indeed, a provocative exercise would be to ask your students (either individually or as a group) to design a game that would avoid typical gender stereotypes (see Reading the Signs question 1). If some students have difficulty imagining such a game, they should discuss why the task is so hard.

Students often enjoy essays about childhood activities; to tap into this interest, Reading the Signs question 1 is a journal entry prompt that focuses on the games students played when young children. As Scanlon points out, board games are part of a pop cultural system that defines gender norms, a system that Naomi Wolf also studies in her selection. Accordingly, question 3 sends students to Wolf's "The Beauty Myth" to compare the games' influence on girls with that of the advertising and the beauty industries. We see as the most challenging question number 4, which asks students to use Scanlon's perspective in a response to Deborah Blum's selection in this chapter. In addition to addressing Blum's argument for the biological basis of gender behavior, students need to consider Blum's personal anecdotes about her own children's play habits.

ANDRE MAYER

THE NEW SEXUAL STONE AGE (p. 512)

We really think Mayer's argument is right on target — and we think you can expect it to trigger a lively class discussion. That's because many students may take issue with Mayer's biting indictment of today's pop culture stars, espcially musicians and singers, who have embraced sexist and chauvinistic gender roles. Often students see these stars, like Mariah Carey or Fred Durst, as cool and cutting-edge, not retrograde, and thus are likely to bristle at Mayer's attack. You might ask your class to list on the board a dozen or so current pop music stars, then consider the images they project. Do they follow the patterns Mayer describes? Alternatively, you could form small groups, each charged with the task of preparing two lists: five current stars who fit reflect Mayer's argument and five who in fact assume more progressive notions about gender. Have the groups write their lists on the board, and then analyze the results. If the lists demonstrate a consensus, discuss the particular details about the artists' images and behavior that led them to be so categorized; if the lists contradict each other, get students to discuss their assumptions about what constitutes outmoded or progressive attitudes toward gender. In either case, you may want to move from observing the phenomenon Mayer decries to addressing its larger significance. Why is a slutty appearance so prized for female stars, even for teen and preteen girls? While a group like Destiny's Child would like its audience to see them as champions of female empowerment, is their choice of clothing, makeup, and hair style really empowering or does it just make them sex objects? How can they account for this trend in pop music?

Students are likely to have plenty to say in response to Mayer's selection. For straightforward argument assignments, try Reading the Signs question 1, which invites students to support or oppose Mayer's central thesis, or number 5, which suggests students debate the degree of chauvinism or liberation that exists in pop music (an in-class debate, in which teams generate lots of specific evidence for their argument, could be the basis of an at-home essay assignment). Two questions narrow the assignment focus, with number 3 asking students to analyze *Maxim* in light of Mayer's charges and number 4 having them analyze the style of female rappers. The most speculative question is number 2, which challenges students to develop their own argument about why the trends that Mayer laments are so prevalent in popular music.

NAOMI WOLF

The Beauty Myth (p. 515)

In this selection, Naomi Wolf describes a fundamental component of our culture's gender mythology: the presumption that women should be judged and valued according to physical attractiveness. Wolf's presentation of this myth is particularly useful in that she distinguishes between biological and cultural imperatives, recognizes the historical fluctuations in this myth, and locates it in the context of power relations. That sounds like heady stuff, but her writing style is clear and direct and students should have little trouble understanding her points. As you discuss this essay, be aware that you may have some students who have struggled painfully with their own physical appearances: They may been tormented by years of failed dieting, they may have a sought a plastic surgeon's solution to a perceived facial defect, or they may be plagued by eating disorders. Although you want to establish a spirit of openness in class discussion, let students know that that openness does not obligate them to engage in confession. If they wish to respond personally to Wolf's essay (and it can trigger that sort of response), Reading the Signs question 1 invites them to do so in their journal (and we recommend that you keep this a private journal entry). One way to address these issues neutrally would be to study the beauty-parlor photo on p. 520: What are the images on the wall, and why are they there? Why does the photographer pose an older woman as a customer?

We particularly like assignments that ask students to apply Wolf's notion of the beauty myth to specific cases. Question 2, which directs them to a local art museum to analyze the representation of women's bodies, could be either an individual or a group project. We've made question 3, which asks students to study a woman's fashion magazine in light of Wolf's argument, a class exercise, but it could make an at-home essay assignment as well. If you prefer an argumentative topic, question 4 invites students to take on one of Wolf's major assertions. And to extend Wolf's thesis, try question 5, which asks students to debate whether men are trapped by standards of physical attractiveness as women are. For this topic, several other selections in the text, including the Diane Barthel (Chapter Two) and Mariah Burton Nelson (Chapter Eight) pieces, could help students generate ideas and arguments.

DEBORAH TANNEN
THERE IS NO UNMARKED WOMAN (p. 525)

This selection proved to be one of the most often used in the first three editions of *Signs of Life*, and we can understand why. In a clear, direct writing style, Tannen looks at nonlinguistic ways in which women are marked in our culture — a topic well suited to lots of lively classroom activities. You could have same-sex groups brainstorm ways in which both genders are marked among, say, students at your school; then you could ask the groups to write their lists on the board. How do the lists compare by gender? Are the lists themselves marked? Because this selection is extremely accessible, students should have no trouble recognizing the specifics of her argument. You may, however, want to spend a little time on her notion of being "marked." Some students may want to complicate her claim that men are normative (Tannen does tend to generalize broadly about males). You could, for instance, ask students to brainstorm ways in which men, too, can be marked — and then talk about how a marked status differs for men and women (see Reading the Signs question 1). This selection is particularly good for analytic assignments that ask students to apply Tannen's notion of marking to evidence they collect themselves (see questions 2 and 3). The final question allows students to use their imaginations in defining what an unmarked appearance for women would be like. We highly recommend that you ask your students to share their proposals with the class!

JAMES WILLIAM GIBSON
WARRIOR DREAMS (p. 531)

At first James William Gibson's selection may seem tangentially related to gender, for he opens with a "war" scene filled with "Communist battalions" assaulting victorious "Americans." But bear with Gibson. You'll quickly see that he's describing not a Vietnam War battle but a fantasy skirmish staged at a *Soldier of Fortune* convention, and you'll see that zeal for this sort of event reflects an increasingly influential model for male gender roles that Gibson dubs "warrior dreams." Gibson's writing is clear and lively, and his method for explaining warrior dreams is perfect for a class emphasizing semiotics and cultural analysis. He takes his reader through a wide range of popular culture, from movies to paintball to warrior magazines like *Gung-Ho*, demonstrating a pattern of paramilitary culture that, he claims, became the "ideal identity for *all* men." Expect that some students who enjoy the sort of entertainment Gibson describes may object to his not-entirely-positive depiction of paramilitary culture; be sure they understand that your use of this essay is to study a cultural systems and mythology and not to pass judgment on their personal lives. Alternately, some students may not have been exposed directly to paramilitary chic, and they might believe that Gibson's talking about a fringe element that has little to do with mainstream society. If you find that's the case, a discussion of 1999's shootings at Columbine High School might help them to see the on-going pervasiveness of what Gibson describes. Students interested in this may enjoy responding to Reading the Signs question 2, which invites them to explore the real-world implications of warrior dreams. In addition, Gibson's selection lends itself to argumentative and analytic topics. Question 1 sends students to Michael A. Messner's selection in Chapter Eight to compare sports ideology with warrior dreams (students should find plenty of parallels), while question 3 prompts students to use Gibson's argument as a framework for interpreting the attractions of professional wrestling. The broadest question, number 4 asks the class to brainstorm current media entertainment aimed at a male audience and then to discuss the prevalence of warrior dreams in pop culture today. Expect your class to compile a long list — one that both you and your students may find sobering.

LAURA MILLER

Women and Children First: Gender and the Settling of the Electronic Frontier (p. 539)

Even students who can't tell RAM from ROM are almost certainly aware of one of the controversies surrounding the Internet: the plethora of seedy and lecherous home pages, sexist diatribes, and pornographic garbage. This sort of material is often clearly identified for what it is, but sometimes it hides under an electronic disguise (for example, "cooking tips" might be a link to child pornography). As a result, many critics have wondered whether controls need to be placed on the Net to protect the innocent — who, in the main, are seen as women and children. Nonsense, says Laura Miller. She goes beyond describing the Net controversy to identify the larger implications surrounding gender roles within the context of American mythology. That is, she takes the common notion of the Net as a "frontier" and does a gender-based analysis of it, ultimately arguing that the calls for protection are themselves patronizing and reflect sexist assumptions. You may want to spend some time in class on her discussion of the "frontier" concept; Laurence Shames's "The More Factor" (Chapter One) could help your students grasp this point. You might also ask your students to consider the typical image of computer afficionados (in films, advertising, and so forth) — it's likely they'll see them as male. Then ask them to consider the implications of this image, for users and nonusers alike.

Your students are likely to have plenty to say in response to Miller's argument. Reading the Signs question 1 invites them to log onto a chat room and then to use their experience to support or to refute Miller's thesis; you might ask your students to do this in mixed-gender pairs so they can incorporate their partner's response into their argument. We highly recommend question 2, which asks the class to stage a debate on whether regulation to protect the innocent is necessary. Teams might first research any legislation on this matter that is before Congress. (We include the photo of a "Take Back the Night" rally on p. 545 to prompt students to consider the differences and similarities between online sexual abuse and the in-person variety. Can students imagine a way in which users can "take back the screen"?) If your students like controversial issues, they might enjoy responding to question 4, a journal topic on the possibility of online rape. Perhaps the most ambitious gender-related topic is number 5, which asks students to interview several women who are Net fans and to use the results of their interviews to argue about the construction of gender roles online. Finally, for a different focus, question 3 sidesteps the gender issue and sends students to Laurence Shames's selection to explain the extent to which the Net appeals to the American desire for more.

Chapter Seven
CONSTRUCTING RACE
Readings in Multicultural Semiotics

We consider this chapter crucial to any writing course with a cultural studies bent, largely because race and ethnicity have become such influential and, sometimes, divisive forces shaping popular culture, politics, education, and even one's personal identity. Race has always been important, of course, but many recent factors — for instance, successes in the civil rights movement, a political and legal backlash against those successes, increased immigration from non-European nations, and increased opposition to such immigration — have heightened Americans' sensitivity to race and racial conflict. Discussing multicultural issues in class can be tricky, especially if your campus has experienced racial tensions or if your students come from ethnic backgrounds that historically have been odds with each other. The potential for in-class conflict is not a reason to avoid the issue; in fact, it's probably the most compelling reason to address it. Students' ability to succeed in school may depend, in part, on their ability to handle those kinds of conflicts, and their writing class may be the only structured environment in which they can explore them.

You'll find that semiotic analysis is an optimal way to handle class discussion of race because, rather than focusing on private passions about race, it addresses the way race serves as a sign for the culture at large. This is not to say that students will feel divorced from discussion of race — indeed, we deliberately ask in the introduction to this chapter "Who are you?" to suggest the potency of race in shaping one's personal identity, and we make that question the focus of the Exploring the Signs of Race journal topic. But even when working on a personal level, a semiotic approach links the individual's views with that of the system, the larger society. The emphasis, then words, is on the cultural mythologies about race that shape our values and our worldviews.

That's not to say that those mythologies may not be changing. Indeed, the United States has passed through many phases in its racial history and, as the twenty-first century begins, it will pass through more. Accordingly, to encourage students to look into the future, the Discussing the Signs of Race question asks the class to consider the implications of an America where there is no majority race (a near-term prediction made by demographers). Since this question is future-oriented, we opted to focus on the present in the Reading Race on the Net exercise. This topic asks students to visit Web sites devoted to the culture of a particular ethnicity and to analyze the breadth of information available. You might want your students to share their findings in class, so they can assemble a composite description of Internet sources on ethnicities.

We feel reluctant to suggest cuts in this chapter, because the selections poignantly speak to the force race exerts both on our personal lives and on the American psyche. The essays do approach the issues from different perspectives, however, and you could choose selections according to those differences. Michael Omi's essay is the lead selection because he provides a broad theoretical overview of racial attitudes and explores how those attitudes are manifested in popular culture. If you've already discussed the media, Omi will provide you with a perfect transition to a unit on race; media focus continues in the next two selections, by Benjamin DeMott on the representation of blacks and whites and by Paul C. Taylor on ethnic crossovers. Jack Lopez follows with a memoir about his youth, when he enjoyed the best of two ethnic worlds; in contrast, Nell Bernstein, bell hooks, and Melissa Algranati next address conflicts experienced by individuals who don't comfortably "fit in" ethnically. Bernstein describes teens who "wear" a new racial identity, as if they were trying on a new pair of jeans; hooks writes a personal reflection that captures the affection a young black girl feels for a doll that is ethnically the same as she; and Algranati addresses the often-overlooked dilemmas faced by mixed-race individuals. Language and culture are the focus of the next selection, in which Fan Shen describes the usually unspoken, socially constituted assumptions governing conventions of writing and scholarship in American universities. Addressing the cross-cultural conflicts he experienced as a Chinese student of freshman composition, Shen's essay is perfect for a writing class. The chapter concludes with LynNell Hancock revealing the social and economic implications of Internet access for race relations in America and Randall Kennedy taking a provocative look at the recent controversy over racial profiling.

MICHAEL OMI
In Living Color: Race and American Culture (p. 557)

We've kept Omi's essay through three editions both for its clear exposition of the prevailing racial beliefs in America and for its focus on how those beliefs are manifested in popular culture. Thus, it is one of the more important selections in *Signs of Life:* it provides a critical framework for analyzing racial issues in selections found throughout the text. Students should find Omi challenging but accessible. Omi does not use the word *semiotics,* but essentially he provides a semiotic reading of race and racial images. His underlying assumption is that cultural myths about race are socially constructed but are seen as natural categories. Race and racism are, of course, sensitive issues, but it's particularly useful to begin class discussion of them with Omi because he focuses on the *process* whereby ideas about race are created, rather than evaluating individuals who believe the ideas. In class, be sure to discuss the concepts he advances for talking about race: overt and inferential racism, unexamined racial beliefs, the ideology of difference or otherness, situation context, and invisibility. Although Omi defines and explains these concepts, the terms may be foreign to students.

The essay lends itself to assignments extending and complicating Omi's analysis of the racial images that prevail in American popular culture. We highly recommend doing Reading the Signs question 1, which asks the class to brainstorm common racial stereotypes and then to discuss how these stereotypes are perpetuated in popular culture. If students have difficulty doing the second task, you might organize their discussion by medium (advertising, movies, and so forth) so that they can more easily focus on particular examples. You can use this discussion to speculate on the media's power to shape our understanding of the world. What difference does it make, for instance, if movies almost always depict gang members as black? What's wrong if advertising presents Asian students as hard-working and industrious? Don't be surprised if someone responds, "But isn't that true?" Such a question, of course, corroborates Omi's claims; we suggest that you invite other members of the class to respond. The remaining topics allow students to examine racial imagery and assumptions in various aspects of popular culture. Question 2 asks them to analyze how race operates as a sign in *Gone with the Wind,* while question 3 has them explore how films such as *Malcolm X* or *Mi Familia* may affect American attitudes toward racial identity. Students can have some fun with question 4, which asks them to analyze ethnicity in an ethnically targeted magazine. Have students work in teams so they can share insights, or ask that they present their findings in class.

BENJAMIN DEMOTT

PUT ON A HAPPY FACE: MASKING THE DIFFERENCES BETWEEN BLACKS AND WHITES (p. 569)

Don't be surprised if DeMott troubles some of your students, for he presents a controversial argument. DeMott deromanticizes Hollywood's tendency to depict friendly race relations, arguing that such fantasy works to perpetuate racial injustice, not to erase it. Students may wonder, "What's wrong with showing cordial race relations? Isn't that better than always depicting conflict?" It's important for students to realize that DeMott laments racial conflict as much as he opposes false images — it's just that he sees the false images as having serious social consequences. Such questions may well lead to a discussion of the effect of film, and the media more generally, on social consciousness. If that happens, you might refer students to Michael Omi's selection in this chapter. Students troubled by the implications of DeMott's position may enjoy responding to Reading the Signs question 3, which invites them to reflect in their journals on the impact of cinematic fantasy, or to question 5, which asks them to describe how they would depict race relations in film.

Whether your students buy DeMott's thesis, they will be able to write several different sorts of assignments in response to it. For a straightforward analysis assignment, try question 1, which asks students to analyze the race relations portrayed in one of the films DeMott mentions (or they can focus on a more recent film, such as *Men in Black II*). The issues this selection raises can be applied to ethnicities and media other than those addressed by DeMott. We've made question 2, which extends DeMott's concerns to other ethnic groups, a discussion topic, but it would be a workable essay assignment as well. Question 4 shifts to catalogues and advertising (you might assign Anne Norton's "The Signs of Shopping" in Chapter One to help students respond to this question).

PAUL C. TAYLOR

FUNKY WHITE BOYS AND HONORARY SOUL SISTERS (p. 579)

Don't let Taylor's hip title fool you: This selection is a challenging, at times philosophical reflection on racial identity and essentialism, ethnic "ownership" of cultural practices, and the tension between authentic and appropriated cultural products. This sounds like heady stuff, but with some help your students should be able to grasp Taylor's ideas about ethnic crossovers in popular culture. You might ask your students to prepare a list of Taylor's most important terms — for instance, cultural nationalism, metaphysical (or essentialist) nationalism, racial obligation, the Elvis effect — with definitions in students' own words. In small groups, students could compare their lists and select the most accurate definitions for class discussion; alternatively, you could collect the lists to determine students' comprehension levels. You could next focus on Taylor's personal narrative frame, his creation as a youth of The Funky White Boys Club, which is the most accessible part of the selection. Ask your students why Taylor is so careful to describe the evolution of his thinking about this club. Then be sure students are aware of the patterns of cultural borrowing that Taylor describes. You can extend his comments about blues and rap to other musical forms that originally were targeted to black audiences but that came to be embraced by mainstream white audiences (jazz and Motown come to mind). This may help students understand Taylor's assertion of the "historically racist trajectory of white American appetites for cultural commodities."

Taylor's selection creates opportunities for thoughtful, challenging analytic assignments. Reading the Signs question 1 allows students to addresses the central question that Taylor poses: whether whites can participate in African American cultural activities. Because your students' success in responding to this topic will depend, in part, on their discussion of specific artists and performers, this topic offers an occasion for a lesson on unsubstantiated generalizations. A somewhat broader topic, question 2 asks students to analyze the possibly racist basis of ethnic exclusivity in popular entertainment and sports. For a comparison topic, try question 3, which invites students to compare the history of rock-'n'-roll with that of rap; they should consider the extent to which each musical genre has gone mainstream and why. Question 4 extends Taylor's concerns to the more general question of preserving one's racial heritage; the Jack Lopez, Nell Bernstein, and bell hooks selections in this chapter can help students respond to this topic.

JACK LOPEZ
Of Cholos and Surfers (p. 592)

We've found that students have never failed to respond warmly to Jack Lopez, and it's easy to understand why. In this accessible memoir, Lopez describes growing up as a Mexican American in East Los Angeles, moving between *cholo* gang culture and the white surfer culture and, in the process, having "the best of both worlds." Students respond positively not only to his message that it's possible both to assimilate and to retain one's native culture; they also enjoy his friendly tone, mild self-deprecating humor, and resolutely nice persona. Students will want to discuss his message about assimilation, of course, but make sure they don't miss some of the subtleties of his narrative. Why, for instance, does his father ask other Mexican Americans if they are Mexican when he knows that they are — and why does that habit so irritate the young Lopez? What's the point Lopez makes about Victor VerHagen, his belligent schoolmate? This selection is also useful if you want to discuss persona and style: How do Lopez's diction and even sentence construction contribute to a reader's reponse?

Because this is a memoir, a natural journal topic is to have students write their own account of how they developed a sense of ethnic identity (see Reading the Signs question 1). A comparison assignment, question 2 asks students to compare Lopez's development of a sense of ethnic identity with that of Melissa Algranati, a mixed-race writer whose own memoir, "Being an Other," appears in this chapter. Lopez's reflections on his father's attitudes toward ethnicity raise the question of generational differences regarding this topic. Accordingly, question 3 has students interview friends and their parents about their sense of ethnic identity and asks the writers to assess the influence one's age can have on such attitudes. This is an ambitious topic, and you may want to prepare students by discussing interviewing strategies in advance. Finally, in describing his move from Mexican East L.A. to predominately white Huntington Beach, Lopez raises issues about ethnic geography and race relations that students can apply to their own neighborhoods (see question 4).

NELL BERNSTEIN
GOIN' GANGSTA, CHOOSIN' CHOLITA (p. 599)

We find the phenomenon of "claiming" a remarkable social trend, and we hope your students are as intrigued as we are. In this easy-to-read selection, Bernstein describes teenagers who "claim," or adopt, a new racial identity. These teens have a variety of motives for doing so. Sometimes they want to emulate friends, other times they apparently want to irritate their parents, and often they just want to seem cool. Ask your class about these motives and whether they had friends in high school (or even now, in college) who were claimers. What does ethnic identity mean to these teens? How is ethnicity a sign for them? Because a few students in your class may be (or have been) claimers themselves, you'll want to make sure the discussion doesn't descend to ridicule of the teens whom Bernstein describes. To avoid that possibility, you might turn to the photo of four teens on p. 598. These people are not necessarily claimers, but they do strike a pose, one that some viewers may consider cool. Ask your students: How do these four teens relate to each other? How would students characterize their styles, and what messages do their styles communicate? In discussing Bernstein, you may want to cover several ethnicities; her essay is valuable in that it covers kids of different backgrounds adopting a variety of new racial identities. They don't claim being white, however, and that's worth discussing, too (see Reading the Signs question 4).

Bernstein's essay creates lots of opportunities for creative and argumentative assignments. Reading the Signs question 1 directs students to stage a conversation between one of the teens and her dad; through role-playing, this exercise could help students see how different generations may read ethnicity differently. The next two questions invite argumentative essays: Number 2 focuses on the media's role in stimulating the claiming trend, and number 3 asks students to take a position on whether claiming is an expression of tolerance or stereotyping (for more on how the notion of racial stereotyping can be slippery, refer students to Randall Kennedy's selection on racial profiling in this chapter). For a more open-ended topic, assign question 5, which sends students to the Jack Lopez selection in this chapter for help in assessing the motives behind claiming.

BELL HOOKS
BABY (p. 605)

If you know bell hooks's work, this selection may surprise you. Rather than engaging in her often-seering analysis of gender and ethnic politics, hooks provides a poignant personal narrative relating her childhood experience with a doll — a brown doll — that looked like her. And students should find this selection quite easy to comprehend. But this is not to say that hooks isn't making a point about ethnic identity: a child needs to see herself reflected in not only her toys but also the culture that surrounds her. Be sure that your students don't overlook that point. Because this selection is short and tightly written, it's ideal for teaching some close reading strategies. You might ask your class why hooks labels herself her mother's "problem child." Why does she say Baby was "waiting" — and for what? Why does she point out that the newest Barbie at the time was "bald"?

Because this is a personal narrative, many instructors may wish their students to write their own reflections on the issues hooks raises (see Reading the Signs question

1 for a journal entry). Yet this selection can be the springboard for interesting analytic assignments as well. Question 2, which focuses on the construction of gender roles, sends students to Scanlon's selection in Chapter Six. (As a corollary, ask students to study the photo of the little girl playing with her doll on p. 606: In what ways is she engaged in role-playing?) To update hooks's reminiscences, question 3 has students visit a toy store and examine the ethnic identities of the dolls sold today. And, to extend the scope of hooks's piece, question 4 prompts them to study the ethnic patterns in other forms of children's entertainment, such as video games. Don't be surprised if your students find examples of extreme stereotyping in videos and toys; Omi's selection in this chapter can provide a useful critical framework for this topic.

MELISSA ALGRANATI
BEING AN OTHER (p. 608)

Algranati's essay is an important reminder of a fact often overlooked in discussions of ethnicity in which supposedly clear-cut terms like *Latino, white,* and *African American* are bandied about. That is, many people in America are not "pure" anything and may find it difficult (or choose not) to identify themselves as a member of a single racial group. How does ethnicity operate as a sign for biracial people? she answers that it's not easy. In this accessible selection, she describes the confusion occasioned by being a Puerto Rican, Egyptian, and Jewish mix — a confusion felt both by others, who expect a unitary ethnic identity, and by Algranati, who struggled with the question "Who am I?" Expect your students to respond positively to Algranati, who neither complains about her status nor indicts the evils of American racism. Instead, she matter-of-factly describes her family and the responses she receives to her mixed identity — and, in the process, creates a sympathetic response in her readers.

Given that sympathy is a likely response, our first Reading the Signs question is a journal topic that allows students to explore their own answer to "Who am I?" This selection creates opportunities for interesting, manageable analytic topics as well. Question 2 asks students to take a stand on whether official documents, such as school applications, should ask applicants to identify their ethnicity; in preparation for this assignment, find out if your college has a ethnic check-off list included in its application form and, if so, what ethnicities are listed. For a topic with open-ended possibilities, try question 3, which asks students how they would identify themselves if they had Algranati's background. For a challenging topic, see question 4, which asks students to assume Algranati's point of view in responding to the claiming fad described in Bernstein's article. Question 5 poses a potentially lively in-class activity; it has the class brainstorm biracial entertainers or other media figures and then discuss the media's tendency to pigeonhole people. What are the implications for people who don't quite fit ethnic categories?

FAN SHEN
THE CLASSROOM AND THE WIDER CULTURE: IDENTITY AS A KEY TO LEARNING ENGLISH COMPOSITION (p. 613)

Even if you don't use any other selection from Chapter Seven, we hope you cover this essay for its analysis of the link between culture and composition. Fan Shen describes the culture shock he experienced when he faced the expectation that he promote the self, not the group, in his writing. In so doing, he describes the ideological basis of Enigsh essay writing — a topic worth discussing with your class even if you don't focus on the multicultural issues. What are the conventions of academic writing, and what sorts of knowledge does it privilege? What's gained by a Western academic approach, and what's lost? Are conventions of English composition essays the same as the writing conventions in other disciplines? But the multicultural issues are significant as well, for in describing his initial expectations about what essays should be, Shen articulates an alternative to the norm with which your students are likely to be familiar. This revelation can create opportunities for students to explore their own expectations as writers; we heartily suggest you assign Reading the Signs question 4, which invites students to examine the aspects of writing that seem "natural" and "unnatural" to them. Indeed, you might raise the issue of how the writing class itself is a culture, one often at odds with mainstream university culture in its concern for student learning.

Shen's description of Western and non-Western styles of learning provides a heuristic that can be useful for a variety of assignments. Reading the Signs question 1 invites students to explore in their journal the extent to which they were raised with a Western concept of self; this question could also be an essay topic. Question 3 first asks the class to discuss whether their classes assume Western learning styles (as did Shen's, we're presuming that for the most part students' classes do). It then asks students to abandon that style by writing up the results of the discussion using the non-Western, or *yijing*, approach. We strongly recommend that, before asking students to attempt this task, you first discuss with them what Shen means by *yijing*; we also suggest that you ask students to read their work aloud so they can discuss how they attempted to achieve the *yijing* style. Question 2 is an accessible topic that asks students to compare Fan Shen's experiences with their own. Here, students could address the impact not only of cultural differences but of gender-based patterns.

LYNNELL HANCOCK

The Haves and the Have-Nots (p. 623)

Some of the most sweeping claims made for the Internet focus on its democratizing potential. The Net, its champions argue, will give all citizens direct access to government, make the fullest libraries available to any student, allow the curious to chat with renowned scientists, and so forth. Is this scenario realistic? No way, says Hancock. In this selection, Hancock outlines some of the very real obstacles to such visions: most important, economics, but also bureaucracy and age. And the lines between the haves and the have-nots often overlap with racial divisions (refer your students to the photo on p. 625 of an African American child using antiquated computer equipment). Some students who believe the "anyone-can-surf-the-Net" mantra will dispute Hancock's concerns, and that's fine. Challenge them to disprove Hancock's point, or, on a more local scale, to research ways in which your community has managed to bridge the gap between the haves and the have-nots. They might interview local schoolteachers or administrators, for instance, to learn the state of computer technology in the local school district — and if there are differences depending on the economic or ethnic status of schools within the district. If they discover deficiencies — which would not be surprising — invite the class to propose solutions (see Reading the Signs question 1). The issue of whether the Internet should be "realistic" also emerges in Hancock's discussion; students interested in this question may wish to respond to question 2 or 4.

We find Hancock's essay valuable for raising the question "Whose world is cyberspace, anyway?" What values and beliefs dominate, and why? We particularly recommend question 3, which asks students to interpret a computer magazine such as *Wired*. Ask your class to study details throughout the publication: the articles, the writing style, the ads, the layout. And urge them to consider the magazine's treatment of gender, ethnicity, class, and even age groupings. Based on our own sampling of such publications, we predict your students will find clear patterns emerging — patterns that, in most cases, will suggest the urgency of Hancock's concerns.

RANDALL KENNEDY
Blind Spot (p. 627)

Post–September 11, we feel it essential that a chapter on ethnicity address that most vexed of controversies, racial profiling. We particularly like Kennedy's treatment of this issue because he avoids the usual simplistic debate over whether the practice is necessary or harmful. Instead, he raises complex questions about the place of stereotyping in our culture and traces the contradictions inherent in the positions of both supporters and opponents. You'll want to make sure these contradictions are clear to your students. Supporters of racial profiling claim that the need to protect the public welfare supersedes the (to them, minor) infringement of individual rights, yet, Kennedy points out, the same people often oppose affirmative action as devaluing the achievement of individuals in favor of a broader social agenda. Opponents of profiling see it as discrimination and argue that race should not be used at all by law enforcement, yet they often support the use of race as a criterion in hiring or school admissions. We suggest that you steer your discussion away from which side is "right," for that question is moot as Kennedy presents the matter. Rather, you might raise some broader issues about the tensions between individual and community rights: when does the one supersede the other? (That thorny dilemma is the focus of a challenging question, Reading the Signs question 4.) In addition, you might encourage them to consider the act of stereotyping itself: When does a valid recognition of a pattern of behavior shade into invalid generalizations? Can there be a difference between "positive" profiling (as supporters of affirmative action would believe) and "negative," and how can we tell the difference? Does it matter who is doing the profiling? (Consider in this regard the habit of claiming as described in Bernstein's "Goin' Gangsta, Choosin' Cholita.") And to what extent does any form of profiling — by law enforcement, by employers, by school admissions officers — presume pure ethnic identities and ignore the multitude of bi- and multiethnic people in this country?

Don't be surprised if some of your students have their own tale about being subject to racial profiling; Reading the Signs question 1 invites students to write a journal entry on such an experience. For an analytic assignment, try question 2, which has students take on the central contradiction that Kennedy finds in the racial profiling debate, or question 4, which prompts them to consider the implications of racial profiling given that ethnic identity in America so often is mixed. The most contentious question is number 3, which has the class debate the merits of ethnic profiling in the wake of the September 11 attacks. Your students should take care to note the range of practices to which this term applies: as Kennedy suggests, a cop stopping a motorist for driving while black may not be the same as a flight attendant confronting a Richard Reid with smoke coming from his sneaker.

Chapter Eight
IT'S NOT JUST A GAME
Sports and American Culture

The academic study of sports did not begin with the advent of cultural studies; indeed, it has long been a mainstay of leisure studies scholarship and education. But while in the context of leisure studies sport is largely regarded as a form of recreation in which amateur participant-athletes play an active role, cultural studies views sports, especially American sports, as a form of entertainment, constituting a major part of what we are calling America's "sports-and-entertainment postindustrial complex." It's a long way, that is, from the neighborhood softball league to major league baseball, where shortstops can pull in quarter-billion-dollar contracts and television producers call the shots, and it is partly the purpose of this chapter to reveal just how far American sports has moved from the recreational playing field to the theatrical spectaculars of mass entertainment. (Striking evidence is that even as sports becomes a larger part of American popular culture, American obesity rates continue to rise.) The Exploring the Signs of Sports in American Culture boxed question accordingly asks students to consider their own relationship to sports, whether they were recreational participants or spectators and fans. If you have student-athletes in your class, you may want to conduct a class discussion in which they can share their motivations for pursuing athletics at the college level. Do they desire to become athlete-entertainers, celebrities who will perform for mass audiences, or do they have more traditional, amateur-oriented motivations? Or are they simply relying on their athletic scholarships to enable them to get a college education?

Whether your students are active participants in sports or passive spectators, they will be aware of the complex cultural codes to which American sports belong. The Discussing the Signs of Sports in American Culture boxed question thus asks your students to discuss the various images that different sports present. In your class discussion you will want to make sure that your students see that these images reflect such larger cultural issues as race, class, and gender. Basketball, for example, has become culturally coded as a black urban sports, while, as David Kamp's piece, "America's Spaz-Time," makes clear, soccer has become associated with the white suburbs. And you'll want your students to consider that athletes are not simply "jocks" (a word, you might point out, that carries its own gendered implications).

The Reading Sports on the Net question asks your students to surf the Net so that they can experience the ways in which contemporary sport has been integrated into a marketing-and-celebrity-driven culture in which consumption and image are everything. Your students could list on the board the Web addresses of the sites that they have found and can describe in the class the content that they discovered there (if you can schedule your class in a computer lab, students can visit and analyze the sites in class). Students can also bring in copies of the sports pages of your local newspaper to enhance a discussion of the similarities and differences between the two media.

As a topic for discussion and critical writing, sports may be a surprisingly controversial, or at least emotional, subject for your students if your university happens to be embroiled in one of the many debates over the proper place of athletics at the college level now roiling America's campuses. Whether the issue relates to Title IX enforcement, which has compelled some universities to cut back their men's programs to make room for more women's sports, or to the question of whether university athletes in such big-ticket sports as football should be paid for their performances, there is plenty of room for spirited debate. Try to make sure that your nonfan students feel free to express what they may think, especially if you teach at a large state university with a high-profile NCAA Division I program. Criticizing, say, the special scholarships set aside for athletes may not be easy in such a context, so you may have to make an effort to ensure an adequate comfort level for all your students.

If your interest in this chapter is primarily related to the current debates over college sports, you will certainly want to assign D. Stanley Eitzen's "The Contradictions of Big-Time College Sport" and Frank Deford's "Athletics 101." A prominent sports sociologist and sports fan, Eitzen takes a rigorous position against what he sees as the "compromising" influence that athletics have on higher education. Offering a rather different perspective, Deford, the well-known NPR sports commentator, advocates allowing college athletes professional status. Though much shorter than the Eitzen piece, Deford's offers a succinct counterpoint that many of your students, especially athletes, will almost certainly appreciate.

If you want to take a social-class based approach to sports, begin with the chapter introduction (especially the Interpreting the Signs of American Sports section), and then assign David Kamp's "America's Spaz-Time" and Henry Jenkins's "'Never Trust a Snake': WWF Wrestling as Masculine Melodrama." Kamp somewhat sardonically explores the suburban world of America's children's soccer leagues (the source of the near-notorious "soccer mom"), critiquing some of the rituals of contemporary middle-class parenting, while Jenkins takes a generally sympathetic, though hardly partisan, look at the largely working-class world of professional wrestling. The Deford selection could be a companion piece as well, for he takes a vigorous swipe at what he sees to be the upper-class-based biases that govern current university attitudes toward the amateur ideal. The selections by Michael A. Messner and Mariah Burton Nelson are essential readings should you focus on gender issues. Messner critically analyzes the role of sports as a male initiation ritual that encodes the patriarchal values of the traditional gender code. If that code drives men to be aggressively competitive, it also values female passivity, a gender trait that Nelson finds all too evident in the world of women's sports, where female athletes are forced to find a resolution to the cultural contradiction of being women in a masculinely defined world. The paradoxes of the apologetic competitor and the athletic fashion plate are just two of the solutions that Nelson critiques. And don't miss the famous, perhaps notorious, image of Brandi Chastain celebrating her winning goal in the 1999 Women's World Cup championship (p. 640). No one would have complained about a man ripping off his shirt in such circumstances; ask your class to interpret the furor over Chastain's performance from Nelson's perspective.

If you are doing a unit on the September 11 attacks, you will want to assign Gary Smith's "The Boys on the Bus," a personal reflection on sports that was written in the immediate aftermath of the disaster. Be sure to have your class look at the image on p. 24 of the September 11 Portfolio of the high school football team streaming onto the field waving an American flag. And if you are including an ethical component in your class study, you could assign E. M. Swift's and Don Yaeger's "Unnatural Selection," which directly and indirectly explores the problem of drug-enhanced athletic performance and the specter of future genetically engineered athletes.

D. STANLEY EITZEN

THE CONTRADICTIONS OF BIG-TIME COLLEGE SPORT (p. 642)

If you teach at a college or university with a high-profile sports program, this reading might lead to some fireworks in your class. From gender inequities, to the compromising (and perhaps corrupting) effects of the commercialization of college sport, to the

IT'S NOT JUST A GAME

low graduation rates of college athletes (especially African Americans), Eitzen sees a world of big-time college sports that comes dangerously close to contradicting the whole purpose of a university. Some students may resent this position, especially if they are athletes, and many, athletes and nonathletes alike, may take the often racially charged position that big-time college sports is the only way out of poverty for some athletes. Be sure to point out that Eitzen addresses this last argument explicitly, suggesting that the promise of riches and fame, especially to African American athletes, is something of a cheat that inhibits their education. More generally, emphasize the high level of empirical detail that Eitzen brings to his work, his statistical documentation and careful sociological research. He isn't just shooting from the hip, and you should make certain that your students understand the value of solid evidence in a debate of this kind.

Two Reading the Signs questions offer your students a chance to find some empirical evidence of their own in support of their arguments for or against Eitzen's proposition that "the pursuit of money has prostituted the university" (question 1) and his questioning whether "the athletic programs at big-time schools [are] consistent with the educational mission of U.S. colleges and universities" (question 2). Questions 3 and 4 each offer opportunities for gender analysis, leading your students to Nelson's and Messner's readings to analyze the role of sports in the construction of gender identities and to debate the Title IX mandates to establish gender parity in college sports spending and participation. Question 5 may be of particular interest to your students if you teach at a college or university that either doesn't have an intercollegiate athletic program or performs at the Division II or Division III level. Endorsing a kind of Division III program for everyone, Eitzen offers an opportunity for your students to discuss the athletic picture at *their* university. Conversely, if you teach at a Division I campus, the question will press your students to imagine what their university would be like without a big-time athletics department.

FRANK DEFORD

Athletics 101: A Change in Eligibility Rules Is Long Overdue (p. 659)

Should you be looking for a college-athlete-friendly piece, this one's for you. Deford not only heartily endorses the professionalization of college sports, he takes a swipe at the university administrators who have held the line on professionalization. Deford's essay should appeal to all of your students for its bouncy brevity as well. If you assign this reading with Eitzen's, you should discuss with your class the difference between the codes of academic analysis (Eitzen is a sociologist) and popular op-ed journalism (Deford is a virtual *Sports Illustrated* icon). Note that Deford relies more on ridicule and anecdote than he does on careful research and analysis. Ask your students whether Deford's comparisons between working professionally at a radio station and playing for pay is really an adequate basis for argument. After all, not every player on a college team is likely to be pursued by a professional "sponsor." You could ask your students to consider the effects on a team if only a few of its members are pulling in thousands, perhaps millions, of dollars. At the same time, your students may find Deford's entertaining, no-holds-barred approach to be more persuasive than Eitzen's careful analysis and argumentation. If they do, ask them to articulate what it is in such a rhetorical approach that makes it effective. If they don't, have them articulate the merits of the academic style.

Reading the Signs question 1 offers your students a chance to write an op-ed of their own and so experiment with Deford's techniques themselves. Conversely, question 2 asks your students to be more like Eitzen, sending them to the library to find evidence for or against Deford's charge that the amateur ideal was constituted in order to keep working-class athletes in their place. Reading the Signs questions 3 and 4 take your students directly to the Eitzen reading, the former inviting them to expand on Eitzen's concerns by imagining the further challenges that the professionalization of college sports might bring to university campuses, and the latter guiding them to a comparison and contrast essay on what both Deford and Eitzen see as the hypocrisies in current college athletics programs.

DAVID KAMP
AMERICA'S SPAZ-TIME (p. 661)

Pardon us for finding David Kamp's piece wickedly funny. With his sardonic take on the way the self-esteem movement seems to have taken over the U.S. Youth Soccer movement, Kamp takes aim at one of the newest sacred cows in American middle-class culture. Of course, if your students grew up playing in a suburban youth soccer league, or are soccer moms themselves, they may not find Kamp so funny. If so, make sure that they see that behind Kamp's barbs lies a serious student and fan of the game that the rest of the world calls football. He's not against youth soccer; he simply has a differerent vision of what it has to offer.

Any discussion of Kamp's article should begin with the overall place of soccer in the context not only of American sports but of global athletics as a whole. One of Kamp's main points is that though soccer, at long last, has taken its place in American culture, it is not only entirely different culturally from the game that produces British soccer hooligans and a well-nigh religious devotion to the sport in fans in the rest of the world, it also differs from most American sports in its unparalleled charge to be both "edifying and nurturing," as Kamp puts it. If you have students from other countries, ask them to share their view of soccer in comparison to the American view. Your students from immigrant communities may have particular opinions about Kamp's focus on suburban (read "middle-class white") youth soccer. Be sure your class understands that for many Americans, especially recent immigrants, soccer has nothing to do with the pieties of U.S. Youth Soccer and is regarded in just the same way as it is in the rest of the world. Thus it would be useful to point out that this article originally appeared in *GQ*. Ask your class how this might have affected Kamp's focus and tone.

Kamp does not ignore the gendered aspects of America's soccer history, and so Reading the Signs question 1 accordingly directs your students to Mariah Burton Nelson to help them analyze Kamp's citation of *Sports Illustrated* columnist Rick Reilly's breathtakingly traditionalist response to the U.S. Women's 1999 World Cup team. Questions 2 and 3 invite a more personal approach, one leading students to reflect on the meaning soccer (or any other youth sport) held for them when they were children, and the other calling for an essay arguing for or against Kamp's provocative assertion that American soccer is "a creepy perversion of a fun game." Question 4 calls for a semiotic interpretation of the place of soccer in the system of American popular and sporting culture. If you are taking a globalist approach to popular culture, you will want to be sure that your students take up the alternative assignment in question 4, which calls for a comparative analysis, contrasting the American image of soccer with that of the rest of the world.

MICHAEL A. MESSNER
Power at Play: Sport and Gender Relations (p. 668)

Be prepared for strong responses to this selection, especially if you have many athletes in class or if your school's sports teams have a devoted following. Messner presents a trenchant analysis of the gender roles that dominate the sports world, finding that an ideology of power and dominance controls the identities of the men who participate in sports. He believes that this pattern is damaging to men and serves to perpetuate social and institutional gender inequities. Although we buy Messner's argument, many students won't and may feel that their (or their friends') values are under attack. If that's the case, point out that Messner is as much concerned about the price athletes pay as he is about describing the dominant ideologies in the sports world. Students may not have thought much about the connection between sports and gender roles; Reading the Signs question 1, which asks them to explore this connection in their journals, can be a good place to start (and may help allay a defensive response). Whether your students agree or disagree with Messner, we've found that this selection can virtually guarantee a lively discussion among your students.

If your students are troubled by Messner's thesis, encourage them to develop counterarguments (Reading the Signs question 5 asks students to stage an in-class debate on his central point). To prepare for their debate, students might interview athletes, nonathletes, and coaches. Although Messner focuses primarily on male athletes, he does mention the place of female athletes in the world of sports; students may prefer to write an argument on this issue (see question 2 and question 3, which additionally raises the issue of ethnic patterns in professional sports). For a text-based assignment, ask your students to respond to question 4, which directs them to analyze the gender roles in a magazine such as *Sports Illustrated*. A reminder: *SI*'s swimsuit issue comes out each February!

MARIAH BURTON NELSON
I Won. I'm Sorry. (p. 679)

Here's a reading that will be especially poignant to your women students, particularly if they are athletes, but be prepared for some defensiveness from males and females alike when it comes to Nelson's questioning of the beauty demands made on women athletes, because Nelson strikes at the very heart of the gender codes that govern the world of sports. Your students may be surprised to realize that they are most comfortable with women athletes who, despite defying convention to the extent of entering what is traditionally regarded as a man's world, still abide by the old gender rules by muting their competitive drives and, so to speak, putting on high heels. You should draw your students' attention to the photo of Serena Williams on p. 681; here Williams appears physically powerful but also undeniably glamorous. (And you might remind them that Williams wore a silver, pearl-studded tiara throughout the 2002 Wimbledon match.) And what connection do students see between the photo of Williams and the 1903 lithograph of two women playing golf (p. 687)? By focusing on such refeminizing strategies, Nelson provides a kind of mirror image of the dilemma described by Diane Barthel in her analysis of the strategies to which advertisers resort when they are trying to pitch products like hairspray, which are traditionally coded as feminine, to men ("A Gentleman and a Consumer," Chapter Two). You might assign Barthel's essay in conjunction with Nelson's as preparation for a discussion of the ways in which those who challenge traditional gender codes often end up reinforcing them at the same time.

Reading the Signs questions 1, 3, and 5 are all useful assignments if your students object to Nelson's contentions. By asking them to observe some women athletes in action (question 1), analyze a women's sports magazine (question 2), or interview women athletes on their campus about the gender pressures they face (question 5), you will be guiding them not only to a sound basis for assessing Nelson's argument but also helping them to appreciate the value of empirical evidence. Question 2 offers a more personal and reflective exercise, which may be especially valued by female athletes, while question 4 presents an assignment in critical thinking and writing that requires your students to consider the arguments of other writers in constituting their own arguments about the role of sports in constructing heterosexual gender norms.

HENRY JENKINS
"NEVER TRUST A SNAKE": WWF WRESTLING AS MASCULINE MELODRAMA (p. 688)

We think your students will love Jenkins's uncondescending yet thoroughly academic analysis of the social significance of the World Wrestling Federation. A topic for semiotic analysis ever since Roland Barthes first tackled it in *Mythologies* (1957), professional wrestling appeals to a paradoxically wide range of fans, from the high-brow crowd who regard it as high-camp hilarity to the working-class men who take it more seriously. It is that latter audience that Jenkins is more concerned with, and his sympathetic analysis of the compensatory spectacles that professional wrestling provides for working-class men in a postindustrial, postfeminist era can be usefully paired with James William Gibson's related analysis in "Warrior Dreams" (Chapter Six). Though it might look like a rather long reading assignment, you might want to assign the Gibson piece alongside Jenkins's to show just how serious the semiotics of the apparently goofy world of the WWF can be.

For a basic exercise in semiotic interpretation, you can assign Reading the Signs question 1, which asks your students to decode some actual WWF contests (make sure your students realize that these are not real competitions but are entirely scripted theatrical productions). Question 2 presents a critical thinking and writing assignment that relates Jenkins's analysis to the larger themes presented in this chapter concerning the role of sport in the construction of gender identities. Questions 4 and 5 offer assignments that call for an analysis of class-based tastes (question 4) and of the way that fandom constructs a sense of group solidarity (question 5). For a more reflective assignment, question 3 provides an opportunity for any serious WWF fans in your class, who may feel embarrassed about speaking up in class, to express in their journals what professional wrestling means to them.

E. M. SWIFT AND DON YAEGER
Unnatural Selection (p. 704)

Beyond the current controversies over the use of performance-enhancing drugs in sports looms the potentially more controversial matter of performance-enhancing genetic engineering. Primarily informational in its approach and effect, Swift and Yaeger's piece nevertheless can stimulate far-ranging class debate, from the specific issue of using biology to get an edge on the competition to the larger issue of the ethics of genetic engineering. At a time when controversies over cloning, stem cell research, genetically engineered food crops, and the potential for terrorists to engineer deadly biological weapons are making headlines, this piece can help your students see how the ramifications of what may look on the surface to be rather trivial can be quite serious indeed.

Reading the Signs assignments 1 and 2 focus on the more limited issue of fairness, with question 1 calling for an op-ed essay about the legality of genetically engineered athletes and question 2 calling for a more personal reflection on the ethics of using genetic engineering to get a competitive edge. Question 3 offers a more imaginative assignment that invites your class to consider not only the possibility of genetically engineered intelligence but the different way in which our culture regards intelligence as opposed to athletic performance (it is our guess that your students will be far more upset by the prospect of artificial "brains" than by artificial athletes; if so, make sure that you discuss the reasons for this). Questions 4 and 5 both call for analytic essays that explore the cultural significance of the use of science in enhancing athletic performance, with question 4 focusing on the values that would lead a society to devote expensive scientific research to the creation of better athletes, and question 5 focusing on an analysis of the cultural pressures athletes face to increase their competitive edge.

GARY SMITH
The Boys on the Bus (p. 711)

Gary Smith's personal reflection in the immediate aftermath of the September 11 attacks may serve as an important reminder to your students of the profound cultural issues those attacks raised. There is no predicting what future terror America may face, but in the months since the attacks, American popular culture has pretty much returned to normal. Smith's piece reminds us of the soul-searching America went through in the dark days of September, wondering whether its obsessive devotion to sports and entertainment was really appropriate in what looked to be a dangerous new world. For that reason alone we feel that Smith's essay is worth assigning. Reading the Signs assignment 1 invites your students to reflect on their own response to the September 11 attacks, and to the changes, or perhaps lack of changes, in their daily routines that the disaster impelled. Question 2 calls for an opinion essay judging whether it was appropriate for Americans to return to popular-cultural business-as-usual so soon after the attacks, while question 3 focuses on the appropriateness of maintaining high school athletic schedules in the wake of the national tragedy. Assignment 4 calls for some critical analysis of four other readings in this text that are devoted to the September 11 attacks, guiding your students to analyze the values that each writer addresses and reflects.

Chapter Nine
AMERICAN ICONS
The Mythic Characters of Popular Culture

Pop culture personalities, media icons, folk heroes. Whatever you call them, America is populated with characters that reflect the nation's dreams, myths, and ideologies. Some may be real people and some fictional creations, but we've found they're perfect for analyzing semiotically. They serve as an accurate mirror of their times, symbolizing the values and interests of the era in which they are created. You can read pop culture characters in much the same way as you do fictional characters from literature. You can ask your students to analyze the values they hold, how they develop or change over time, how they compare with other characters, how they capture the hearts of their audience. And because such characters so closely reflect the interests of their culture, they create opportunities for addressing a host of serious issues such as gender, class, and ethnicity. Some of the very best student writing we've received has focused on popular characters. Perhaps it's the novelty of looking at culture in the same way one might look at literature; perhaps it's the immediacy of the subject matter; or perhaps it's the fun of exploring and explaining "people" who inhabit our daily lives but tend to be taken for granted. Whatever the reason, studying popular characters can be a fine way to develop your students' analytic skills while having some fun in the process.

The boxed questions in the introduction are designed to inspire a spirit of fun and serious critical inquiry in your students. We encourage you to try the Discussing the Signs of American Characters question, which asks the class to brainstorm a list of their favorite pop cultural icons and then to analyze the list. Not only will this question get all your students to participate, but it asks them to consider the cultural and social basis for their personal tastes. The Exploring the Signs of American Characters question is also personally reflective, asking students about the significance that characters from children's television had for them when they were young. The Reading American Characters on the Net exercise invites your students to look outward at the larger culture's values — and at America's cult of the celebrity — by investigating the role the Internet plays in fostering a celebrity's status. In doing so, your students may see how both the celebrity's image and an audience's response to that image are careful media constructs. Alternatively, you could ask students to investigate the backgrounds of historical figures that resonate in the American imagination; check **http://www.biography.com** for twenty thousand or so entries.

Because the chapter's introduction does the work of setting up a critical framework for analyzing characters, you could easily allow your students to pick which essays they'd like to read if you don't have time to cover them all. Michael Eric Dyson starts off with an analysis of a real-life superhero, Michael Jordan, with the next two selections, by Gary Engle and Andy Medhurst, focusing on fictional superheroes, Superman and Batman. A trio of selections on toys and games follows, with N'Gai Croal and Jane Hughes explaining Lara Croft, Emily Prager turning to the doll industry to critique Barbie, and Gary Cross moving from Barbie to G.I. Joe. Mark Caldwell returns to real life in his review of the queen of domesticity, Martha Stewart. In a humorous piece, Roy Rivenburg examines characters who have been used to peddle everything from cereal to paper towels. Jenny Lyn Bader follows, exploring whether today's twentysomethings can even believe in heroes anymore — a comprehensive essay that's crucial to include even if you use the chapter selectively. To conclude the chapter, Tim Layden provides an answer to Bader by recalling the firefighters and law enforcement officers who struggled to save whoever they could on September 11, 2001, and the days following.

A number of selections focus on toys as objects of analysis. Some students might wonder why: after all, isn't college where you study "serious" subjects? Our response: Toys are very serious business. In childhood we are conditioned to accept our culture's dominant mythologies, and toys and games are one of the primary "teachers" of those beliefs. We feel it essential that students see that dominant beliefs aren't "just in the air"; they are embodied in cultural artefacts that we usually take for granted. Toys aren't just fun; they help shape some of our most fundamental belief systems.

American mythmakers have not created an abundance of positive female pop culture characters. There are a few, but when asked, our students (both male and female) tend to think only of sex symbols, advertising characters (who are usually either a mom or an Elvira type), and romanticized historical figures such as Betsy Ross. Just as the introduction raises the issue of race, we suggest you ask your students about gender also. Why have female characters been limited to such a restricted range of roles? Are things changing? What sort of female characters, real or fictional, would your students like to see assume a greater role in American popular culture?

MICHAEL ERIC DYSON

BE LIKE MIKE? MICHAEL JORDAN AND THE PEDAGOGY OF DESIRE (p. 729)

This selection provides an opportunity to teach students the need to keep in check personal responses to a subject as they attempt to analyze it. Often in class discussion of American characters, Michael Jordan's name has come up, and with good reason. Not just a sports hero, he has an extremely attractive public persona (distinct from the bad-boy image of so many other athletes); details of his personal history, such as his father's murder, are tragic; his on-again, off-again retirement creates an aura of mystery and suspense. But expect your students to stick to a functional explanation for Jordan's popularity: "He's so much better than any other basketball player!" "He's just amazing!" If your students are Jordan fans, fine. They could benefit from this selection, though, because Dyson goes beyond the functional explanation to probe the cultural mythologies surrounding this larger-than-life hero. Dyson's unambiguous admiration for Jordan may be useful for students who resist analysis of their pop culture favorites because they equate analysis or criticism with negative commentary. And, to us at least, Dyson's argumentative base is sound: he locates Jordan within the context of black participation in sports, for instance, and he examines other parts of the system in which Jordan can be interpreted, including advertising and consumer culture. Some students may be put off by Dyson's rather academic style, but the diction is relatively jargon-free and students should grasp most of his points.

This selection creates opportunities for a variety of analytic and argumentative topics. A straightforward assignment is Reading the Signs question 1, an argument topic that focuses on one of the complaints about Jordan that Dyson mentions (note that it's not one that Dyson shares). For a more challenging question focused on ethnicity, try question 2, which has students respond to the belief, to which Dyson alludes, that basketball is primarily a black form of cultural expression. Students might do some research on the history of basketball for this topic; they'll find that the sport was invented by a white man. If you want your students to focus their attention on sports more generally, assign question 3, a class discussion prompt that gets students thinking about why sports personalities have become America's heroes, and question 4, an essay prompt that addresses Dyson's claims about athletics as a means for facilitating "white male bonding." For this last question, students should consult Messner's "Power at Play" in Chapter Eight.

GARY ENGLE
What Makes Superman So Darned American? (p. 738)

This is a long selection, but it's clearly written and gives your students plenty to talk about. Engle's thesis is that Superman has succeeded as a superhero because he embodies a mythology dear to a land of immigrants. Superman, Engle asserts, has not just gone from rags to riches but has moved from being an alien to a quintessential American. That such an debatable thesis is well defended and thoroughly argued makes the selection a winner for class discussion. Why does Superman seem more patriotic than Batman? (If you want to pursue the "What is an American?" angle, Reading the Signs question 4 asks students to take on Engle's claim that Superman is more American than John Wayne.) Students would do well to consider whether the view of immigrants is always as romanticized as Engle suggests, either in our own era or in past decades. Engle here is asking that essential semiotic question, "Why Superman?" If your students don't buy his argument, ask them to propose alternative answers to the question "Why?" (Reading the Signs question 2 allows students to argue with Engle's thesis). If they don't see Superman as really being that important a character, again ask them why. Here, the fading of the assimilationist ideal in our multicultural era comes into play; Reading the Signs question 1 invites students to address this issue.

    Engle's selection also works well when combined with other readings. Reading the Signs question 3 sends students to Robert B. Ray's definitions of heroic types (Chapter Four). Although Engle says little about race and gender, those issues are certainly relevant to Superman's success, so question 5 suggests that students consult the Michael Omi (Chapter Seven) and Holly Devor (Chapter Six) selections as they consider the significance of these issues. And finally, question 6 invites students to view a *Superman* movie to see if film has altered the comics' depiction of this superhero.

ANDY MEDHURST
Batman, Deviance, and Camp (p. 746)

We find Medhurst's essay to be a lot of fun — and we hope you and your students do as well. Of course, Medhurst has a serious point to make: for him at least, the original Batman-and-Robin duo was gay, and it was the homophobic wave of the 1980s that eliminated Robin from the spate of *Batman* movies. Students often resist this thesis — they have real difficulty accepting the notion that such a popular character, and one intended to entertain children, could be homosexual. Medhurst uses a nice blend of evidence to support his claims, however, so challenge your students to refute that evidence if they dislike his argument (rather than simply denouncing it). Be sure they note his creation of a historical context, especially his discussion of Fredric Wertham's *Seduction of the Innocent* — skeptical students tend to find this discussion to be the most persuasive part of Medhurst's argument (Reading the Signs question 2 asks students to critique Wertham's argument). Discuss too Medhurst's reading of individual scenes from the 1960s *Batman* TV series. It's best if you can arrange to show at least part of a *Batman* episode in class; in fact, Reading the Signs question 1 suggests that students view tapes of the show in preparation for arguing for or against Medhurst's thesis. Check your college's media library to see if they have file tapes of old shows. One term that many students don't quite understand is *camp*; that's a central concept in Medhurst's essay and you may want to spend some class time discussing it. For a topic addressing *camp*, see question 4, which sends students to Susan Sontag (whom Medhurst discusses in his selection) for some further research. To bring Medhurst's argument up to date, question 3 asks students to buy some current Batman comics and to explain his current sexual orientation. As students work on this question, be sure they consider who the audience for comic books is and how that might affect decisions about Batman's sexuality.

N'GAI CROAL AND JANE HUGHES
LARA CROFT, THE BIT GIRL (p. 761)

Is Lara Croft a feminist model for girls to emulate? Or is she just a cyberBarbie? Let your students decide. In this accessible piece originally published in *Newsweek*, N'Gai Croal and Jane Hughes profile this virtual character and the reasons she has attracted so many fans. Ask your students whether she indeed is a "strong" woman, as some proponents claim, or simply a sexy body operating in a sexy technoevironment. And have them analyze the photo of Lara on p. 762: How is she depicted, and for whom? Ask them to locate Lara Croft within the larger context of female characters as well: How does she relate to a figure like Xena or Tank Girl, or to reach back a bit in time, Wonder Woman? Why is it that boys are among her most ardent fans (not so with Tank Girl)? For this last question, don't accept as an answer the fact that boys predominate in the videogame crowd: There have been plenty of attempts to launch female characters, but most have flopped. To ask that familiar semiotic question, why Lara?

We've created a variety of questions to accompany this piece. The first Reading the Signs question allows students to reflect on Lara's success in their journals; you could make this an essay topic as well. Shifting the focus to style, question 2 asks students to examine this selection as an instance of journalistic prose. For argumentative topics focused on gender, assign question 3, which poses the feminist-icon-or-cyberBarbie debate that we mention above, or question 5, which prompts students to interpret the gender roles in the film *Tomb Raider*. Question 4 shifts to male videogame characters and has students analyze the gender roles such games impose on them. Don't worry if you're not familiar with such characters: we're always surprised at how fluent our students are in the latest of videogame fare. Aren't they studying?

EMILY PRAGER
OUR BARBIES, OURSELVES (p. 766)

Toys are much like cartoons. Students may never have stopped to think about the toys they played with as a child, but when they do, the sparks start flying. In fact, this accessible and clearly written selection has never failed to generate a lively discussion in our classes, and it has been one of instructors' favorite selections in the first three editions of this book. Prager takes a tongue-in-cheek look at Barbie and the role this doll has played in shaping the gender expectations of millions of children. Be sure that students recognize Prager's tone and discuss how it contributes to their response to it. Some students may respond defensively to this essay; when they perceive part of their upbringing to be under attack, they may feel they're under attack, too. They may want to do Reading the Signs question 3, which asks students to explore in their journal the significance of their Barbie doll to them as children. It's important that students notice that Prager includes herself, as a child, among Barbie's fans and that she distinguishes between the doll and its designer — whom she heartily attacks — and the children who play with it. If you had a Barbie once, you might want to confess the fact so students won't feel as if you, too, are judging them.

The assignments that you can generate with this essay will show your students that they can write serious analysis and have some fun at the same time. Be sure to analyze the photo on p. 767: How is Barbie continually being adapted to appeal to new generations of children? We highly recommend the first Reading the Signs question, which asks students to bring a toy to class and discuss its significance, first in same-sex groups, then with the whole class. Not only does this question broaden the issue beyond Barbie, but you can ask students to interpret the gender-related patterns in the whole class's collection of toys. Question 2 allows students to be more reflective, asking them to interpret a toy they played with as children. If students are not persuaded by Prager, they may want to respond to question 4, which allows them to consider how Jack Ryan, Barbie's creator, would defend himself against Prager's charges. The most challenging question is number 5, which sends students to Laurence Shames's "The More Factor" (Chapter One) to explore Barbie's consumerist ethos. Be sure your students visit a toy store as part of their research for this question; they'll find that Barbie's possessions are no longer limited to a car and a condo.

GARY CROSS
BARBIE, G.I. JOE, AND PLAY IN THE 1960S (p. 769)

This is a perfect companion piece to the Prager selection, for while Gary Cross discusses Barbie (and she occupies first place in his title), his main concern is G.I. Joe. What we like about this selection is that Cross charts Joe's shifting fortunes as cultural and social attitudes change — a perfect instance of the semiotic principle that a sign's meaning is historically conditioned. For an even broader cultural context, also assign bell hooks's short piece in Chapter Seven, "Baby," for an ethnic slant on these issues. As Cross points out, G.I. Joe eventually failed in his creators' attempts to adapt to changing times: How does he compare with the action-adventure toys in toy stores today?

You might also compare Cross's analysis of Barbie's appeal with Emily Prager's, since the selections differ substantially in tone, style, even substance (note that Cross attributes a different origin to Barbie than does Prager; we believe Cross is accurate). Which selection do they find more persuasive, and why? How might the intended audience affect each writer's presentation? This selection also raises gender issues: what's an appropriate toy for a girl or boy? Reading the Signs question 4 is a class exercise that would generate a lively discussion of this question.

You'll see that our questions for this selection push students to consider toys as culturally significant objects. Reading the Signs question 1 seems simple — it asks students to invent a toy of their own — but the challenge is writing an essay explaining the rationale for the creation. Be sure to assign this second part, because that's where the hard thinking (and perhaps rethinking of the design) comes in. For a topic that brings Cross's issues up to date, assign question 2, which asks students to survey current action-adventure toys and to analyze them in terms of the warrior dreams framework that James William Gibson describes in his selection (Chapter Six). We encourage students to see the larger cultural role that toys play in socializing kids to mainstream beliefs; question 3 invites them to address this issue.

MARK CALDWELL
The Assault on Martha Stewart (p. 775)

As we write these words, Martha Stewart is under greater attack than Caldwell imagined when he wrote this piece, what with Kmart in bankruptcy and allegations of insider training plaguing the reigning queen of domesticity. What is it about Stewart's creation of a lifestyle industry has made her so popular that she's become, as Caldwell puts it, a "national symbol"? Is it the sheer ubiquity of her products, both actual and media? What does Caldwell mean by the "democratizing of good taste"? That point is especially important, because it is the key to Caldwell's explanation for Stewart's iconic status. Most students should be familiar with Stewart's industry, but if they're not, bring to class her magazine, *Living*; a videotape of Stewart's daily TV appearances, or a tape of her weekday radio broadcast (the schedules for both conveniently published in *Living*). Alternately, a visit to **www.marthastewart.com** will fill them in.

You'll find it easy to create focused, manageable assignments based on Caldwell's selection. We suggest several questions that prompt students to interpret Martha Stewart products directly: Reading the Signs question 1 asks students to analyze an issue of *Living* to see if it indeed has a democratizing effect, while question 3 sends them to a local KMart to examine the in-store Stewart display. For an investigative topic, try question 2, which asks students to interview Martha Stewart fans as the basis of their own arguments about her appeal. Perhaps the most challenging question is number 4, which sends students to "The Addictive Virus" in Chapter One and has them consider the connection between Stewart's popularity and Americans' increasing fondness for material goods.

ROY RIVENBURG
Snap! Crackle! Plot! (p. 780)

In this pleasantly tongue-in-cheek selection, Roy Rivenburg, a humor columnist for the *Los Angeles Times*, "investigates" the private lives of advertising characters such as Mrs. Paul and Mr. Clean (be sure to discuss the image of Mr. Clean on p. 784). In the process he notices a number of surprising patterns. Few characters, for instance, are married. Ask your students why that might be so, especially given that food products, which commonly are associated with a character, have a domestic function. Expect this selection to trigger a discussion of the power of advertising: Are consumers really so influenced by promotional characters? We strongly recommend Reading the Signs question 1, which asks the class to brainstorm and categorize as many advertising characters as they can (don't worry — while Rivenburg mentions lots of characters, there are plenty more out there). Be inventive with the categories, and study issues such as ethnicity, class, and gender. What patterns emerge? What do those patterns say about America's values and ideologies? If your students have resisted a semiotic approach thus far, this exercise ought surely to win them over.

We see Rivenburg's selection as ideal for either analytic or creative assignments. For an analytic research topic, question 2 asks students to investigate the controversy surrounding Joe Camel, that cigarette-peddaling creature who finally was retired as part of the tobacco industry's settlement with the federal government. Question 3 gives students a chance to be creative, asking them to invent a new representative for one of the products advertised in the second chapter's Portfolio of Advertisements. As an alternative, you could ask students to pick an ad of their own and then create a new character to represent the product. Finally, question 4 asks students to interpret the Taco Bell chihuahua.

JENNY LYN BADER
Larger Than Life (p. 785)

We highly recommend that you include Bader's essay in your syllabus, no matter how many other selections from this chapter you cover. Unlike the other selections, which interpret particular characters, Bader takes a broad view and contemplates the meaning and availability of mythic heroes for her twentysomething generation. Bader should strike a chord in many of your students, because she essentially argues that heroes no longer have a powerful influence over today's younger generation and that what is needed are realistic role models. This position should inspire plenty of debate among your students, who are likely to disagree with each other on the validity of Bader's thesis (Reading the Signs question 2 invites an argumentative essay in response to Bader's central argument, and question 4 triggers an in-class discussion of traditional American heroes). If you have nontraditional students in your class, take advantage of their perspective and ask them whether they believe Bader's position applies to older generations as well.

Bader's argument is likely to touch some students personally. Consider assigning the journal topic mentioned in question 1, which allows students to explore à la Bader the heroes they admired when they were young. They may also enjoy question 3, which invites a creative response to Bader's call for "stories of spirit without apology." Bader's essay lends itself to direct analysis topics as well as more imaginative ones. Question 5 asks students to analyze Michael Jordan using Bader's perspective, but students could easily substitute another sports figure or a political figure if they prefer. Finally, question 6 has students consider Bader's argument in the light of the September 11 attacks on America, an event that caused many Americans to rethink what constitutes heroism.

TIM LAYDEN
A Patriot's Tale (p. 795)

This short selection from *Sports Illustrated* is a perfect companion to Jenny Lyn Bader's piece, for while Bader questions whether heroes can exist for her generation Layden suggests a new category of hero: people like the New York City firefighters who risked their own lives to save victims of the September 11 attacks on the World Trade Center. What's interesting about Layden's article is that, early on, he focuses not on the firefighters themselves but on a brother of firefighters, a right guard for the New England Patriots who, by virtue of his profession, would be a typical candidate for the status of "hero" or "star." Ask your students: What is the attraction of professional sports players? What is it about them that prompts so many fans to idolize them? Then move to the description of the player's three brothers, the firefighters who worked the WTC disaster. What is the effect of the first-person narration? Why does Layden include it? And how does Layden attempt to redefine our sense of who a hero is? You'll note that this piece is designed to trigger an emotional response in readers, and you should discuss that with your class. Does that add to or detract from Layden's overall message?

It remains to be seen whether America's apparent redefinition of heroes endures. The favorite costume for Halloween, 2001, was a firefighter's uniform. Will that trend prevail? Reading the Signs question 1 invites students to investigate this question. For a stylistic analysis, assign question 2, which asks students to analyze Layden's rhetorical strategies. The most complex question, number 3 has students argue whether the firefighters and other rescue personnel would satisfy Jenny Lyn Bader's call for "a new pantheon" of heroes.